Criti

MA

"Because the Margaritaville of his well-known song is a desultory place, readers may not be prepared for these good-natured tales of free-spirited characters. . . . In fact, Mr. Buffett's lighthearted endorsement of adventure is so persuasive that, upon finishing the book, many readers will be tempted to get out their maps."

—*The New York Times Book Review*

"Buffett's songs—and now his short stories—are peppered with romantic images of heaving blue seas, swaying palms, and sand the color of the grains in that lost shaker of salt he sang about in his hit 'Margaritaville.' "

—*Orlando Sentinel*

"Refreshing . . . From the freezing wilderness of a Wyoming ranch to a hair-raising cruise in the lush waters off the Florida Keys, Buffett takes the reader on a rousing tour of the United States."

—*The Monitor* (McAllen, TX)

"Buffett pays loving tribute to the Gulf Coast in accounts of local superstitions, character sketches, sea adventures, humorous anecdotes. All are told in a laid-back style reminiscent of the oral tradition; collectively, they create a vivid image of time and place."

—*Library Journal*

TALES FROM MARGARITAVILLE

Fictional Facts and Factual Fictions

Jimmy Buffett

FAWCETT CREST • NEW YORK

A Fawcett Crest Book
Published by Ballantine Books
 Published in the United States by Ballantine Books, a division of Random House, Inc., New York, and simultaneously in Canada by Random House of Canada Limited, Toronto.

Library of Congress Catalog Card Number: 89-92588

ISBN 0-449-22248-9

This edition published by arrangement with Harcourt Brace Jovanovich, Inc.

Manufactured in the United States of America

First Ballantine Books Trade Edition: October 1990
First Ballantine Books Mass Market Edition: August 1993

With the exception of the four autobiographical stories in the ''Son of a Son of a Sailor'' section of this book, *Tales from Margaritaville* is a collection of fiction. Names, characters, places, and incidents are either the product of the author's imagination or are used fictitiously. Any resemblance to actual persons, living or dead, locations, or events is entirely coincidental.

To

J. D. BUFFETT,

who took me to baseball games where I first heard
the roar of the crowd and loved it;
and to MARY LORAINE PEETS BUFFETT,
who taught me to wonder what lay
beyond the Alabama horizon

—J.B.

CONTENTS

CONTENTS

Son of a Son of a Sailor

Write what you know about.
—MARK TWAIN

Changes in Latitude

WALKABOUT

"Somehow I picked up an image of those 'tame' Blackfellows who, one day, would be working happily on a cattle-station: the next, without a word of warning and *for no good reason*, would up sticks and vanish into the blue.

They would step from their work-clothes, and leave: for weeks and months and even years, trekking half-way across the continent if only to meet a man, then trekking back as if nothing had happened.

I tried to picture their employer's face the moment he found them gone.

He would be a Scot perhaps: a big man with blotchy skin and a mouthful of obscenities. I imagined him breakfasting on steak and eggs—in the days of food-rationing, we knew that *all* Australians ate a pound of steak for breakfast. Then he would march into the blinding sunlight—all Australian sunlight was blinding—and shout for his 'boys.'

Nothing.

He would shout again. Not a sound but the mocking laugh of a kookaburra. He would scan the horizon. Nothing but gum trees. He would stalk through the cattle-yards. Nothing there either. Then, outside their shacks, he'd find their shirts and hats and boots sticking up through their trousers. . . ."

—BRUCE CHATWIN, *The Songlines*

The Aboriginal people of Australia believe the earth was sung into creation and is held together by songlines or dreamtimes, and every so often in a person's life, he will get the calling to go "walkabout" as was so superbly described by Bruce Chatwin in the passage above.

I am not in the frame of mind these days to do so, as I still have a little too much attachment to the toys that tie me to modern life. Still, the old saying in South Florida of a decade ago—"He who dies with the most toys wins"—becomes less of a credo.

Besides, if I just did like the bushman and walked out of my Patagonia shorts, T-shirt, and flip-flops, leaving them in a pile on Highway A1A, and started walking naked up U.S. 1, I would be on the six o'clock news in every city in America by the time I made it to the seven-mile bridge.

Being your own boss and having a phony-baloney job like I do affords me the great excuse of saying "I have to be alone and free from distractions in order to create." It's basically a line of bullshit, but I do find exotic places tend to cultivate more exotic tales. Anyway, I recently said good-bye to Key West and packed my three bags for anywhere in the world. I had everything I needed: music, fishing gear, cotton clothing, and good books.

I stopped briefly in Los Angeles, where I appeared on the "Tonight Show" and played a few songs after Tommy Lasorda got through plugging his pasta joint in the Valley, and Johnny Carson was the last American I talked to before boarding the Air France flight that night for Tahiti.

My need to be alone had carried me halfway around the world to the island of Bora Bora, which had haunted me since I saw *South Pacific* performed by the Catholic Theater Guild in Mobile, Alabama, when my piano teacher played "Bloody Mary" and sang "Bali Ha'i" with a strong southern accent. She hooked me on the myth and planted the seeds of discovery that eventually led me to the South Pacific.

I checked into my favorite waterfront bungalow at the Bora Bora Hotel, away from the noisy honeymooners. I had a fine welcome-back dinner at Bloody Mary's and chatted with old friends.

The big news on the island was the arrival of a space cult. Some people had purchased one of the outer islands, and they were waiting to be picked up by a UFO and taken to "out there." But according to their information, the extraterrestrials who were running their shuttle would not land in a place where a lot of human remains were buried. Once a week they put on a little show for the tourists where they prayed and showed off the latest fashions from outer space, and we arranged for a boat to take us out to see the spectacle.

The morning of our trip, however, I came down with a relapse of breakbone fever, a cousin to malaria transported around the tropics by man-eating mosquitoes. My malaria attack was accompanied by a strange, low-pressure cell that covered the blue Pacific sky with a dense curtain of gray and dumped monsoon rains on the island for a week.

I wrote between fever spells, hot and cold flashes, and visits to the island pharmacy where I bought cough syrup from a beautiful lady behind the counter. She made being sick seem somehow worthwhile.

I had plenty of snake dreams that week, the kind that rip through your mind like Velcro being pulled apart, and I tried to write down all of the oddest things. I examined my scribbled notes one morning, and as I listened to the pissed-off tourists swimming in the rain, I knew it was time to start getting all this stuff on paper and write the book I had put off for a decade.

I left the island in a panic—the international date line had robbed me of a full day. I was due in Australia on Friday morning, and Friday was Thursday in Bora Bora. I was on a plane to Sydney without even being able to say au revoir to the beautiful lady at the pharmacy, and I never met the space people.

Damn, I do detest losing a day for no good reason at all. Back in my wilder periods I used to lose lots of days, sometimes weeks, but that was because of my own lack of discipline. Just to cross some imaginary line on the globe and be told that it is now Friday when a minute ago it was Thursday just doesn't seem fair, even if you eventually get it back.

The concert tour had me bouncing around Australia like a kangaroo, playing an opera house one night and a waterfront dive the next—which, looking back, was quite funny. Most loathsome events become humorous tales with the passage of time. In trying to explain to reporters why he laughed when he heard the term, *H-bomb*, Lord Buckley used to say, "Humor is the absence of terror and terror the absence of humor."

I was back in America last December with newly discovered books. *The Songlines* by Bruce Chatwin and *Echoes of the Dreamtime* by Ansle Roberts were a few of the new things I brought with me.

One of life's great pleasures is exchanging good books with close friends. I gave a copy of *Dreamtime* to Ed Bradley, and he promptly took me to a bookstore in Aspen where he bought me a copy of Joseph Campbell's *The Power of Myth* as a birthday present.

I read the book, digesting it slowly like a crème brûlée, and made my New Year's resolution to start my own book—which now seems ages ago as I sit here on the island of South Bimini two weeks before my deadline typing my ass off so this book will be published in September, and my editor won't lose her job.

There seem to be a lot of responsibilities that I didn't comprehend when I decided to pursue this new career, but in the words of Tully Mars, a man you will soon meet, "Hell, Columbus thought Cuba was China." But that seems to be true of life in general, at least on this planet and in this lifetime, which is the only one I am halfway familiar with.

JIMMY BUFFETT
April 17, 1989
Bimini, Bahamas

WHERE IS MARGARITAVILLE?

One of the questions I am asked most is, "Where is Margaritaville?" I answer, "When you are there, you will know it."

I have known about it for quite a while. Ever since I was a child, I have had a recurring dream of visiting an island; it appears at different locations on the perimeter of the Gulf of Mexico—west of Tortuga, south of Ship Island, or in the middle of Perdido Bay. Somewhere and everywhere, Margaritaville has its origins.

I remember my grandparents' backyard in Pascagoula as my first base. From there, I ventured out into the world. A very narrow tributary bordered the property, and my cousin and I mounted many pirate expeditions down the bayou that emptied into the Mississippi sound. We would set up camp down by the old Coast Guard station and fish and watch oceangoing vessels making their way past Horn Island, out into the blue waters of the Gulf. I imagined myself at the wheel of a freighter heading out to sea, and I let my mind go where my feet couldn't yet carry me. After an exhausting day of playing pirate, I went to bed with my grandfather's old world atlas open across my chest after I had traced imaginary sea routes from that muddy little bayou in the backyard to the exotic places of the world.

I have visited many of those places with the names that sounded so intriguing, and I have always carried with me that floating island of my dreams. The legend of Attiragram, the wonderfully loony inhabitants of Snake Bite Key, and the cast of characters I have encountered during my trips on so many boats may hold some clue as to where Margaritaville is, making the quest to find the mythical island the real adventure.

So now join me, if you will, on the real and unreal voyages to and from Margaritaville, wherever the hell it is.

The Heat Wave Chronicles

TAKE ANOTHER ROAD

Tully Mars was lost in space. His conscious mind was a thousand miles away in the trade winds, where white sand beaches and coconut trees were surrounded by the crystal clear sea. His subconscious, however, was still in Wyoming. His horse knew where Tully was going and trotted along through the snow without needing any direction from the worn leather reins.

Tully dismounted near the edge of the Snake River. Mr. Twain, his fail-safe sorrel stud, stayed put. The cattle had broken through again, and fence posts lay in the fresh snow. Tully checked the tracks of the stray Herefords and examined a fresh cowpatty.

"They ain't far," he said aloud. "Like everything else, just follow the bullshit."

He mounted Mr. Twain and loped across the downed fence line and up the north hill. From a stand of small pines on the ridge, he spotted the cows huddled together near the fence by the road.

"Another couple of minutes and I would have had to put their pictures on a goddamn milk carton," he said. He moved toward them and started laughing at the thought of a Gary Larson cartoon.

"Car!" he yelled at the cows. They looked at him like he was crazy.

"At least this is real cowboy work," Tully said to Mr. Twain. "I swear this is the last year I am cowboyin', Twainny. I ain't cut out for dude ranch shit. We're going to the ocean, me and you."

Tully Mars had been a cowboy all his life. He was the descendant of an old Confederate great-grandfather, who had come from Tennessee to Wyoming after the Civil War. He founded the town of Heartache, Wyoming, named for the woman who promised to follow him West but never did. Tully's side of the family was not destined to be included among the land barons of the Old West. His father and grandfather before him preferred a simpler life of horses and solitude.

His Uncle Travis's side of the family had bought this land, and Tully worked for Travis since he was a kid. But Americans were now eating more dead plants than dead animals, and the cattle business in Wyoming was feeling the health craze. Frustrated and tired, Tully's uncle had just sold the ranch to a syndicate from California and had moved to Arizona.

Mrs. Thelma Barston, the junk-bond queen, was the principle owner. She had blasted onto the property two days earlier in a jet helicopter. Her entourage included several lawyers and accountants, a hairdresser, a masseuse, and a tall man in a white mink coat who looked a little light in his loafers. Tully watched them climb out of the chopper, holding their noses as they passed the stock pen—it was obvious that the new owner of the Double M Ranch was more interested in designer jeans, tax write-offs, and toy poodles than in ranching.

Mrs. Barston reminded Tully a lot of Cora Brown, an ex-beauty-shop-operator-turned-cattle-baroness from Schenectady who he'd seen in a movie called *Rancho De Luxe*. The film had been shot fifteen years ago up in Livingston, Montana. Tully had ridden his horse all the way through Yellowstone Park up to the film location just to get a look at his hero, Slim Pickins, the man who rode the H-bomb in *Dr. Strangelove*.

Tully wound up working six weeks as a stand-in. The director said he bore a striking resemblance to Jeff Bridges, the star of the movie. He also had his first real affair—with the set designer, a beautiful lady from Maui. She tried to get him to come to California, but Tully knew this was as close to Hollywood as he ever wanted to get.

Tully ran the cows back through the hole in the fence. Snow began to fall again. He stabbed at the frozen earth with his pick, and, with a surgeon's touch, made quick work of the mending job. He twisted the barbed wire in his frigid hands and thought about that beach again, for though he'd been a cowboy all his life, Tully Mars was also a man of the sea.

He hadn't a clue as to where his fascination with the ocean came from. When he was a child, he had practically memorized *Treasure Island* and never missed an episode of "Adventures in Paradise" on the old black-and-white TV—watching Gardner McKay steer the schooner *Tiki* through the South Pacific.

When the movie *Donovan's Reef* came out in 1964, he hitchhiked all the way to Denver, which was the closest place it was showing. For two days he watched John Wayne and Lee Marvin swagger through French Polynesia, fighting, loving, and drinking Tahitian beer from giant brown bottles.

The manager of the movie theater finally reported him to the police as a missing person, and he was put on a bus and sent back to Wyoming. Those had been the two big adventures in his life, and since then he hadn't left Wyoming once.

Tully cut cows five days a week, got drunk on Saturday night at the Twisted Steer Bar, and spent all day Sunday in bed at Limited Love, the local whorehouse, reading about the rest of the world. Up until now, he had been pretty content just to dream about faraway places, but his fortieth birthday was coming, and he was beginning to wonder if he would ever actually get to see more of the world. Plus, the Wyoming winters were finally getting to him, and the sale of the ranch was not a good sign.

He drove the cows back through the snow to the small corral next to his Airstream trailer, which sat in the middle of a circular field surrounded by aspen trees. He had painted it to resemble a pink coral reef. Tully drove the cows across the snow-covered field and felt as if he were on top of some giant cake, gliding through white frosting toward the candy in the center. His flock of plastic flamingos perched near the corral made it feel even more that way.

One small Hereford shied away from the rest of the herd. Tully and Mr. Twain were of one mind and moved to cut the angle between the calf and the tree line. Then Mr. Twain went to work, moving back and forth like a cat, edging the stray back to the gate. Tully loved this cutting horse, his only true friend in the world.

Except for Limited Love, women were scarce in these parts unless you were into the skiing crowd down in Jackson Hole, but Tully thought it communistic to stand in long lines for anything, especially if it cost thirty dollars a day to slide down a mountain on boards. Besides, he was too old to date.

He closed the gate, unsaddled Mr. Twain, led him into the shed behind the trailer, and called it a morning. He was not looking forward to the afternoon; he had been called to the main house for a meeting with Mrs. Barston.

Tully lay in his rope hammock, wrapped in an electric blanket that was plugged into a one-hundred-foot extension cord attached to a portable generator outside. It was the only way to stay warm because the heat had gone out in the trailer. He snored loudly, dreaming about his elusive island—now high up in the Andes in the middle of Lake Titicaca.

He ran through the jungles of Peru trying to catch a voluptuous Incan sun princess who carried fresh fish from the seashore up to the mountain kingdom of Cuzco for the Inca himself. Try as he might, Tully could not catch her; he was wearing an outlandish pair of shrimp skin boots that weighed a ton.

He finally got the boots off and was now running faster, closing in on the maiden. Suddenly he was attacked by a pack of vicious poodles. They snapped at his bare feet, and the naked princess disappeared into the jungle.

Tully woke to the distant, high-pitched cacophony of

barking dogs and the annoying whine of a snowmobile. He climbed out of his hammock and walked to the porch. The tall man in the white mink coat was almost at the door. Behind him a pink snowmobile towed a little trailer in which half a dozen yapping poodles sat shivering.

"You are late. Mrs. Barston has been waiting for you, Mr. Marsh." His voice was like a snake's hiss.

"Mars, bud. The name is Mars, and with the attitude you seem to be glued to, I'll send your ass to the angry red planet without a rocket," Tully snarled.

If this was going to be a showdown, it was certainly far from the classic frontier confrontation on a deserted street. No, this was the late twentieth century. The man from California stood in the snow, wrapped in a mink, while the human burrito from Heartache waited for a reaction.

Tully hoped the man wouldn't want to fight. He really had no interest in coming out from under the electric blanket and exposing himself to the elements. No doubt this would harm him more than it would harm the man in the mink coat.

"Tell her I'm on my way, Bruce."

The man's tight face relaxed for a moment. "How did you know my name, Mr. Mars?" he asked politely.

"It seemed to fit, son."

Tully went back inside and turned on his Sears portable TV. He combed his hair, dusted off his boots, and watched the last part of "World Championship Wrestling" to get himself in the mood for the meeting with Mrs. Barston. He figured she was the kind of woman who would approve of Ted Dibiasee, the million-dollar man, and his tactics. Tully knew this was the *real* showdown, and he gulped a shot of rum before he bundled up and set off for the corral.

The temperature seemed to be dropping a degree an hour, and the wind was starting to pick up. He and Mr. Twain ambled slowly down the road toward the big house. It had been the main thoroughfare in his life. Yet instead of riding directly to his meeting, he rode up into the woods to a lookout that dated back to Indian times. It was his rallying point—where he always came when he needed to think.

He and Mr. Twain stopped when they reached the top of the giant flat boulder, and Tully stared out at the vista before him. The blowing snow just about obscured the view he knew so well, but he could easily remember it by thinking back to a warm spring day when he had spent the afternoon up there with a beautiful woman from Florida he had met in the Million Dollar Cowboy Bar in Jackson Hole. They drank Goombay smashes on the boulder and did the limbo under the Western sky.

Thelma Barston did not want to look her age and was lucky to live in a time when liposuction, silicon implants, and collagen injections had allowed plastic surgeons to totally disprove the theory that you could not make mountains out of molehills.

Tully had left his lookout and was now watching Thelma from the apple orchard just above the main barn. A huge new glass-walled addition to the house held a pool and a gym. Thelma was doing aerobics in a pink leotard that looked two sizes too small as Michael Jackson's ''Beat It'' shattered the peace of the valley.

''If that spandex outfit rips, she could take out the

whole town,'' he said to Mr. Twain. Tully heard the rumble of large trucks double-clutching and looked down to the highway below. Three Global Van Lines, semis with California plates, chugged up the hill to the house.

" 'The time has come, the walrus said,' " he proclaimed and nudged Mr. Twain toward the ranch.

Tully knocked on the freshly painted pink door and was greeted by another new face—the housekeeper, no doubt. "Oh, you must be the furniture man. I'll get Mr. Bruce."

"No, I am *not* the furniture man. Tell Mrs. Barston that Mr. Mars is here to see her."

The little woman looked confused and stuttered, "One mo—moment, one moment."

Soon Bruce was at the front door, and his sour attitude had returned now that he was back on home turf. "Wait here," he ordered.

Tully mockingly snapped to attention. "Yes, sir," he said and clicked his heels.

Now, Tully had grown up around this great old ranch house that his uncle had built, but today he felt he was on another planet. The pastel walls were completely bare, and there wasn't a stick of furniture in sight. Tully strolled around and remembered the Indian portraits and photographs and rugs that had always filled the old ranch with a sense of history.

"Smells like a fucking hospital," he muttered.

"Beg your pardon?" The hiss behind him was familiar.

Bruce motioned that Tully was to follow him to the workout room. A large woman with a definite pencil-thin moustache was kneading a long white body on a massage table. Two men in black Armani suits came into the room and stood by the big window.

Thelma Barston rolled off the table. She wrapped herself in a large white towel, but not before Tully caught a glimpse of her new, large pointed breasts as she stood up.

"Welcome, Mr. Mars. I'm glad you could make it. We've been waiting for you."

Bruce brought her a bottle of Perrier, and she sipped and paced back and forth in front of the large window. "Mr. Mars, I will get right to the point. Cattle and ranching are not profitable investments anymore. The West is changing, and we have to change with it, or we will all be extinct, like dinosaurs and Indians."

"Excuse me, ma'am," Tully interrupted, "but there still are a few Indians around."

"Thank you for the information, Mr. Mars. Now may I continue?" she asked sharply.

"It's your soapbox, Thelma," Tully said.

"Mr. Mars, we are a landholding company. We are not interested in cows. We are going to make a few changes around here. We are going to be more efficient. We are going to run this ranch as a profitable business." She snapped her fingers for the maid, and the little woman brought the pack of pint-size pink, black, white, and gray yap dogs to her. "And we are going to breed poodles. This is our breeding stock, Mr. Mars. These are the animals that you will be taking care of from now on if you plan to continue working here."

She paused to straighten the rhinestone collar on the pinkest poodle and continued. "Our research indicates that poodle ranching is on the verge of becoming the fastest-growing segment of the pet industry. With the current baby boomer's boomlet, parents are buying pets as never before, and our promotional plans will ensure that a poodle will be next to every playpen within five years.

"In addition, our research shows that employee productivity increases dramatically when the corporation demands higher health standards and an attractive environment. Consequently, you will be required to attend exercise class regularly, and that hideous eyesore of a trailer has to go. We will provide you with new, sanitary accommodations in the employee housing building, which we plan to build within the next six months."

Thelma's passionate speech about profitability left her breathing hard, and the towel began to slip down, revealing her heaving cleavage. She stared at Tully with her emerald green contacts and asked, "Do you get the picture, cowboy?"

Tully looked around the room. Then he walked over and picked up one little black poodle and said, "I don't think we're in Kansas anymore, Toto." The poodle jumped down, and Tully pointed at Bruce. "Is he gonna be the daddy dog?"

Bruce came unglued and lunged at Tully, who laid him out with his free hand. The maid stifled a laugh, and Bruce crumpled like the Wicked Witch of the West. "Who do you think you are? The Marlboro Man?" he screeched from the floor. "I could sue you for this. You backwoods, racist, sexist redneck. You'll never work in this business again!"

"Well, ma'am," Tully politely said to Thelma Barston, "I appreciate your view of the New West, and I hope you have a wonderful time trying to change things.

But I do believe it is time for Tully Mars and his trusted horse Mr. Twain to blow this fucking pop stand.''

He lifted the heavy massage table and hurled it through the picture window. ''Fresh air, Mrs. Barston, smell that fresh air!'' He stepped carefully through the broken glass to where Mr. Twain was standing, mounted quickly, and galloped off to the trailer.

''Too much stuff,'' Tully sighed. He gazed at all his worldly belongings in the Airstream and began to pick up stakes. No doubt the law would be at his door any moment.

He packed a few pairs of jeans and his favorite cotton shirts, a pair of flip-flops, the Dry-as-a-Bone raincoat he ordered from Australia a few years ago, an old stainless steel Colt .38 pistol, a bamboo fly rod, ten of his favorite cassettes, all of his Travis McGee paperbacks, the *Ocean Almanac*, and his first-edition copy of Mark Twain's epic travelogue, *Following the Equator*, a gift from his father. He also packed one piece of rare art—his old Martin 0–18 guitar, which had been painted by a crazy artist fellow he had met up in Livingston who had gone on to become famous. He stuffed it all into an army duffel bag and threw it into the cab of his '51 Chevy pickup truck.

He loaded Mr. Twain into his horse trailer, dug a sleeping bag and his two-man tent out of the shed, and tossed them in the back. The old truck fired up immediately, and Tully never looked back. He was taking his pony to the shore, and like many travelers before him, he did not really have any idea what route he would take or where he was really going.

Tully headed north on Highway 89 through Yellowstone Park and made it to Livingston, Montana, that night. He drove up through Paradise Valley to the house of his crazy painter friend but found a note on the door saying he'd gone fishing in Key West. It sounded like the place to go, and Tully wrote it down.

He spent the night at Chico Lodge and ran into some people who had worked on *Rancho De Luxe*. They stayed up most of the night drinking margaritas and telling stories. The next morning, using his road atlas, he finally managed to start plotting his way to the tropics.

Tully Mars looked at the big picture and realized just how far he had to go to get to the ocean. He would head for the Mississippi River and take a right toward New Orleans. The Gulf Coast of Alabama looked interesting. That might be the place to try to find passage to the islands of the Antilles.

He fed Mr. Twain and loaded him back into the trailer and spent most of the day on Interstate 90, driving east through Montana. Just out of Billings, the road signs were full of information about the Custer Battlefield. Tully decided to have a look. He could do whatever he liked—at least as long as his three-thousand-dollar life savings held out.

He turned off the interstate and drove through the Crow reservation up Highway 212, following the signs to the Custer Battlefield. There weren't too many tourists in the dead of winter. When he pulled into the visitors' center, one of the park rangers came over to say hello and have a look at Mr. Twain.

The ranger's name was Joe McCormick. He was originally from Tennessee but had been a Custer fanatic all his life. Now he was where he belonged, doing what he truly loved. Tully felt the same way, so Joe took Tully through the museum and into the vault, where he showed him a pair of Custer's buckskin pants.

Tully was overcome with a strange sense of awe as he toured the exhibit rooms and then the battlefield. The weather had broken, and the sun lit up the snow-covered grounds. That night, the two men had dinner together in Hardin and talked cutting horses, politics, and Custer. They ended up back at Tully's motel room with a rousing rendition of ''Garryowen,'' which Tully played and Joe sang.

''Meet me at the visitors' center tomorrow morning at sunrise, and bring your horse. There's something I want to show you,'' Joe said before he left.

Tully lay in bed and thumbed through *Following the Equator*, stopping at several of his favorite stories. He read for about an hour and then put the book down.

Tully realized that he, too, was on a journey—one that might prove just as exciting as those he had read about for so long. He knew no other person in the world who had so completely and swiftly ended a long phase of life and set out to find a better one. He was alone but happy, and he had a sense that this was an adventure that needed to be recorded.

He picked up the notebook he had bought that day in the Indian store and turned to the first page. He would start a journal. In large letters he printed: Take Another Road—One Cowboy's Story Of His Search For A Better Place. He turned off the night light and dropped off to sleep, falling into the island dream that had been a part of him as far back as he could remember.

MARCH 15, 1989

I met Joe McCormick this morning at the visitor center of the battlefield and to my pleasant surprise he came riding up on a beautiful painted pony and told me to saddle Mr. Twain. I had gotten up early and read the brochures about the battlefield so that I had a sense of direction about the place but I still couldn't quite figure out why the myth of the Battle of the Little Big Horn fascinated me. For a long time my idea of what went on here came from a movie called "They Died With Their Boots On" in which Errol Flynn played the General, and then there was the painting in the Twisted Steer above the bar back in Heartache but now I see that there is more to the story. Heroism and tragedy, brashness and humiliation, victory and defeat, I guess it's the culmination of the culture of the American West. It is a place where you sort of lose yourself in time. Anyway Joe McCormick told me that this was sort of against regulations to be taking civilians around on horseback so if anybody asked, I was doing research. We rode off East up to the high ground and there was not a living soul in sight but I could feel the ghosts of the Seventh Cavalry and the Indians all around me and I had goose pimples all over my body. It was spooky but at the same time damn exciting to be riding Mr. Twain through such a place. Joe was giving me a blow by blow description of the way the battle shaped up as we headed up to Weir point where we looked down on the cottonwood trees along the Little Big Horn River and I tried to think of what it must have felt like to have been one of two hundred or so men looking down on thousands of pissed off Indians. It must have been like stepping in a bed of fire ants and then just standing there. We rode up on the high ground to where Major Reno retreated, eventually was joined by Captain Benteen, and held out until the Indians took off the next day. I had this strange feeling as we rode that I had been there before. I sort of knew where I was going or maybe it was Mr. Twain who had been there before. Anyway we rode down to where Reno crossed the Little Big Horn and first charged the Indians. It was great, Joe started talking in cavalry lingo and we went from a walk to a trot and then he shouted another order and we were charging toward the cottonwoods and went at a full gallop until we came to the highway and the railroad tracks near the little Gary Owen post office. Tears were streaming out of my eyes and my moustache was frozen solid. Mr. Twain was snorting and sidestepping and then Joe McCormick turned to me and said "You won't see that kind of shit in a Marlboro ad." I laughed and said that was one hell of a way to start your day. We then rode quietly through the site of the Indian camp and I was in my own movie. I could feel the ghosts of the Oglala and the Northern Cheyenne. We followed the supposed trail that Crazy Horse took to outflank Custer and came upon the markers in the snow that showed where Custer and his brothers had fallen. We didn't talk much for there wasn't much to be said. It was a place to feel, lots of energy there. Finally Joe spoke and said "You know the Indians around here call us park rangers the Ghost Herders.'' We rode back to the parking lot and I brushed and fed Mr. Twain and loaded him up, thanked Joe McCormick for his hospitality and told him I would write him when I got to wherever it is I am going. I went in and bought a couple of books and a patch for my jacket and then got back on Interstate 90 finally heading South to Sheridan and knew that somewhere out on that old battlefield, I had come pretty close to talking to God, whoever he is.

Tully Mars
Custer Battlefield

Tully whistled the tune to ''Garryowen'' over and over for about five hundred miles during the drive south to Denver. He didn't know anyone there, but he remembered the time he had run away to the big city. The policeman who had taken him to the bus station had felt sorry for him and bought him the best chicken-fried steak he had ever eaten. Then he put Tully on the bus back to Heartache.

Tully drove for what seemed like forever down East Colfax Avenue trying to find the place—it was a diner and a motel on the outskirts of town, owned by an old prizefighter.

He was just about to give up when he caught a whiff of mesquite smoke and remembered the name of the place.

''The Pig and Whistle!'' Tully shouted and hit the gas pedal.

It had been swallowed up by the sprawling city, but the Pig and Whistle was just as he remembered. Tully sat in one of the Naugahyde booths and ordered chicken-fried steak with white gravy. He had been waiting twenty-five years to eat it again. He did like his mom had told him long ago and chewed slowly—not so much for digestion but for pure enjoyment. The clientele talked about another disappointing season for the Broncos and then got distracted from football by a fender bender out in the street.

After lunch Tully found a feed store in Aurora and bought a bag of oats for Mr. Twain. He stopped at a rest area to take advantage of the mild afternoon and rolled his sleeping bag out on a picnic table to catch a speed nap. When he woke up, he unloaded Mr. Twain and went for a long ride, and then he brushed him down.

Smog hovered above Denver like a yellow curtain, and the majestic Rocky Mountains lined the horizon beyond.

He could tell bad weather was on its way from the buildup behind Pikes Peak. Tully Mars had lived in the mountains all his life and knew you could only appreciate their real beauty from a distance.

Now he was headed for Hannibal, Missouri, the home of Mark Twain, but Kansas stretched endlessly to the east.

He had waited until nightfall so he wouldn't have to look at the monotony of the flatlands, and he drove and drove through the night. The wind picked up and caused the trailer to fishtail behind him, and a heavy snow started to fall.

He stopped at a truck stop for coffee and first gave Mr. Twain a little exercise walking around the parking lot in the snow. Then he loaded his horse back into the trailer.

Inside, Tully was amused by the waitress's T-shirt. Across the front, it read:

> Auntie Em,
>
> Hate you, Hate Kansas, Took the Dog.
>
> Dorothy

The storm was the sole topic of conversation in the greasy spoon as weary travelers came and went.

Tully pressed on, but he had to drive at a snail's pace for about three hours. At last the whiteout forced him to the side of the road. He bunked in with Mr. Twain in the trailer and wondered if he would ever get out of Kansas and the snow.

The next morning he had to climb through the hay door of the trailer and dig out of a three-foot snowdrift before managing to get back on the road. He was still in Kansas for most of the day, but the worst of the storm had passed, and by late afternoon he finally saw the skyline of Kansas City. He checked into a motel just across the river from the airport and slept well into the next morning.

Tully woke up around noon and turned on the TV. The news of the day centered on the effect the big storm was having on traffic in town. He decided not to move that day.

MARCH 17, 1989

No wonder Dorothy had such vivid dreams. The last twenty four hours hasn't been exactly a day at the beach but I plowed on through a blizzard thinking about where I was going and listening to my Bob Marley Anthology. I guess I am destined to dine on Bar-B-Q on this leg of the trip and I found a great one just outside Kansas City called Haywards. I picked up a couple of extra bottles of sauce for the road. It's not that I don't like seafood, but I met a guy back in Jackson Hole once who told me that he made a living by cherry bomb fishing. He would drop his mini-depth charges into the Snake River and then gather up the shell-shocked catfish, filet them and chop them up with a cookie cutter and sell them to the restaurants up in Yellowstone as sea scallops. I will wait until I can see the ocean and then I will feast on seafood.

Mr. Twain doesn't like Kansas any more than I do. We rode down a plowed street by the river, but for the most part he has been cooped up in the trailer. The snow was piled high all around Kansas City so I went to a big shopping mall and spent the whole afternoon just wandering around and singing the words to Wilbur Harrison's song. I guess a lot of other people had that in mind cause the place was packed. I tell you it was something. I counted seven stores that just sold ice cream and four that just sold frozen yogurt to people who would die from eating too much ice cream. America truly does have something for everyone. I stopped in a travel agency and talked to a very pretty girl with a deep tan who had just come back from the Virgin Islands. She gave me some brochures and wished me luck on my trip.

There was a movie theater that showed four

movies at once and I went to all of them. The last one was a rerun of E.T. which I loved the first time I saw it. I was sitting there crying into my Dr. Pepper when E.T. was about to croak under the oxygen tent even though I knew he wasn't going to die, but I wasn't alone, the whole theater was blubbering and then this little girl sitting in front of me turned to her mother and shouted "Mommy he can't die, we are in Kansas, they should call the Wizard." I got out of the movies around midnight and the weather had cleared and the moon was up so Mr. Twain and I finally had a decent ride and I brushed him out twice as long as usual. He seems to be holding up fine all things considered. The man on TV said traffic was back to normal so next stop Hannibal, Missouri, and check off "visit Mark Twain's Home" from my endless list of things to do.

T.M.
Kansas City

The only good thing about the endless trek across Kansas was that it made Missouri go by in a flash, and Tully was dying to see the Mississippi River. It would be a milestone, the turning point in his trip to the tropics.

The big storm had moved rapidly ahead of him, leaving clear skies and cold air in its path. He took Highway 24 toward Hannibal and arrived there shortly before noon. Just outside town, Tully found a stable where they taught riding lessons. At first the woman who ran the place didn't believe it when Tully said his horse's name was Mr. Twain. But after he told his story, she let him unload Mr. Twain and gave him a pasture all his own—free for the whole day. Tully rode his horse for almost two hours before he said good-bye and headed off. He turned onto Mark Twain Drive at the Tom and Huck Motel and drove through the little town, more and more dismayed at the overkill of his hero.

Signs pointed to the Mark Twain Home and Museum, the Mark Twain Village Shoppes, the Twainland Express Depot, the Mark Twain Motor Inn, the Tom Sawyer Diorama, and the Huck Finn Shopping Center. He finally made it to the bridge and pulled over so he could look out on the muddy Mississippi. To the south he could see Jackson's Island, and he felt the urge to go find Tom and Huck.

He looked down into the brown water and saw a log floating along with the current. A big frog was sitting on the log, and he wondered what the world looked like from that vantage point.

"How far you headin' there, Mr. Frog?" he shouted out, but the frog paid him no mind.

Tully watched the log until it slipped around a bend out of sight and then he went back to town. He got mad at the way Mark Twain had been made into a tourist attraction, but then he reconsidered. Mark Twain was a hero to a lot of other people besides Tully Mars. Ernest Hemingway, who was a pretty fair wordsmith himself, had said that American literature began with *Huckleberry Finn*.

He wondered how many people who came here had ever read one of Mr. Twain's books.

Tully walked through the streets of Hannibal with his head down. He was thinking very seriously about what all this meant. What if all the wonderful places that had filled his imagination back on the ranch all turned out to be theme-park images of things that didn't even exist anymore? What if there was no desert island where he could run Mr. Twain up and down the beach in the low tide?

He had burned all his bridges back in Heartache and didn't know a soul within a thousand miles of where he was standing. He might wind up lost in the world, sleeping in the snow on a park bench like the people he saw in Kansas City.

This depressing stream of thoughts suddenly stopped when he collided with a large immovable object. Tully lay in a daze and looked up to see bronze figures of Tom Sawyer and Huck Finn towering over him. He studied the look on their faces and began to laugh loudly. He wiped the trickle of blood from his nose.

"One for the river pirates!" he yelled at the statues.

MARCH 19, 1989

I do believe that if Mark Twain had never drawn a breath, the Hannibal Missouri Chamber of Commerce would surely have invented him to support the tourist economy. I am now propped up in my tent at the Mark Twain Cave and Campground, the sole occupant of a stand of oak trees near the Cave where Tom, Huck and Becky Thatcher used to play. I sort of have the place to myself right now. It doesn't really open until Memorial Day whenever that is, but the manager was quite impressed with the fact that I had named my horse after the most famous man in these parts. This was the second time today it happened. I saddled up Mr. Twain and took his kids for a ride. We rode over to the cave and went inside. I could see how your imagination can go wild in such a place. It is quite warm here to me though the local people look to be still in the grip of winter. I figure being the acid tongued devil that he was old Samuel Clemens would not look favorably upon what the local population has done in his name, maybe he would laugh and just ask for his share of the money. "Human pride," he said, "is not worthwhile; there is always something lying in wait to take the wind out of it." Anyhow, tonight life is grand and I am tucked in my sleeping bag staring up at the stars on the banks of the Mississippi River, the bookmark of the American continent. This side is the West and a mile away is the East and tomorrow is another adventure and I am starting to like my new life.

T.M.
Mark Twain Cave and Campground
Hannibal, Missouri

Tully was singing along with Bob Dylan as he sped down Highway 61 toward Memphis on a beautiful morning. The weather had been improving steadily, and an early hint of southern springtime filled the air. The little run-in with Tom and Huck had put him back on the road to adventure again.

He had eaten grits for the first time in his life that morning at the Chat 'n Chew Cafe near Blytheville, Arkansas, served to him by a very pretty waitress named Donna Kay, who was astonished at the thought that someone had lived nearly forty years without grits.

"Why, those taste buds of yours are in for a world of

surprises if you are goin' to New Orleans, honey. I used to live down there."

She told him to be sure to stop at the Acme Oyster House and slurp a dozen for her and try the brisket sandwich at Tujague's.

"You ever been to Graceland?" he asked her.

"No, I ain't. I've always been meanin to get down there, but I just haven't found the time. I've heard that most people in this country have never been more than twenty miles from where they live. I'd like to find somebody like that to marry, 'cause the two husbands I had rarely came within twenty miles of home. You ever been married, cowboy?"

"Naw," Tully answered, "I haven't found the right girl yet."

"Now let me just guess," Donna Kay said. "Wanted: One beautiful blonde with big tits and a great personality. Must be into horses, willin' to travel and do whatever she is told and not talk back. Preferably with a trust fund that would allow her and her new husband to live a life of leisure. Am I close?"

Tully chuckled and poured more syrup on his biscuit. "How'd you know?" he asked.

"Women always know before you tell them."

"You have any idea where I should start lookin' for the future ex-Mrs. Mars, Donna Kay?" Tully asked.

"You just said it, honey: Mars." Donna Kay walked down to the register and rang up a breakfast order, and when she came back, Tully was already on his feet.

"You know, ahhh, this is the most I have talked to anyone, except Mr. Twain, that is, I mean a human or a girl for that matter, since I left Custer's Battlefield. And I was wonderin', since you used to live down in

New Orleans, maybe you could give me a few more tips as to what to do when uh, you, uh, I, uh, get there,'' he stammered.

''Maybe I could meet you down there, cowboy. I need to get out of here anyway. I got a night off, and all this high-spirited talk of travel you been dishin' out sort of got my gypsy soul all wound up,'' she said.

She wrote her number on a napkin and handed it to Tully. She looked at him and smiled. ''I think I can tear myself away from all this excitement around Blytheville. I know a gentleman when I see one, and I still got a few friends living in the French Quarter who can be counted on for a good time. You go on down to Graceland and see Elvis, and call me tomorrow from wherever you are.''

MARCH 21, 1989

I spent the afternoon at Graceland and then found a little diner called the Cupboard that Donna Kay had told me about and had a plate full of turkey and dressing, lima beans, and blackberry cobbler and being of sound mind and full body I figured it's time to do this.

The Last Will and Testament of Tully Mars.

I leave my trusty horse Mr. Twain, my trusty 1951 Chevy pickup truck and trailer to Donna Kay Dunbar care of the Chat 'n Chew Cafe in Blytheville, Arkansas. My books I leave to the Heartache, Wyoming, Public Library in hopes that they will inspire others not so happy about their lot in life to do something about it. There will be no money left as I plan to spend it while I can, and when I die, I would like to be buried under a palm tree on the beach in an unmarked grave away from the maddening crowds like I saw today at Elvis' grave.

T.M.
Memphis, Tennessee

The plump little waitress offered Tully more iced tea while he finished writing, but he politely declined and went to use the pay phone.

Donna Kay answered, and Tully was glad to hear her voice.

"So how was your visit to Mecca, cowboy?" she asked.

"Are you going to be able to meet me in New Orleans?"

"Yes, I am. I found a flight tomorrow morning that gets me into New Orleans about two. How was Graceland?"

"I'll tell you about it when I see you," he said.

MARCH 22, 1989

I was rudely reminded of the fragility of life on earth tonight on the outskirts of Yazoo City, Mississippi. It was raining quite heavily, but the truck was cruising right along and then I saw the wreck. Blood on the highway as the old country song said. A station wagon full of women on their way home from the garment mill had collided head-on with a pulp wood truck. The police hadn't arrived but several other cars had stopped to help the women trapped in the car. I had seen dead people before, but all of them were old with the exception of the one man who got shot at the Twisted Steer in Heartache by a jealous husband, but I had never seen so many dead people and parts of dead people before. We managed to pull two of the women still alive out as the police and paramedics arrived, and I hope to God that they do survive. There really isn't much you can do for dead people, and I believe that when your time is up, your time is up. I felt worse for the living relatives who began arriving and realizing what had happened to their loved ones. I know I had some second thoughts about this whole thing of running off back in Hannibal but the only good thing to come out of what I saw tonight was that it made me realize how short our time here is and they will have to drag me kickin, whoever it is that comes and tries to take me from this world. I am meeting Donna Kay in New Orleans. I like her a whole lot.

T.M.
Mississippi

Tully and Donna Kay sat at a small table in Tujague's sipping rum drinks under a photograph of Harrison Ford. Next to him, in the picture, the owner of the restaurant was holding a big plate of chicken.

Tully had meandered toward the Crescent City, driving down the old canopied River Road, hoping the beauty of Spanish moss dangling from four-hundred-year-old oak trees would help him forget the horrors of the previous night.

He stopped on the way into town and found a horse

farm where they would take good care of Mr. Twain. Then he drove to the airport and picked up Donna Kay. She could tell right away from Tully's somber mood that something was bothering him.

"You wanna tell me about it?" she asked.

"Yes, I do," Tully promptly answered. He told her all about the wreck.

"It was terrible, Tully, but you couldn't do anything about it but what you did. Life is just too short, and people die every day. You just happened to see death up close and personal, and it's not a pretty picture."

"Okay." Tully took Donna Kay's hand.

"Now I don't want to be your therapist or anything like that, but I spent a lot of money and busted my ass to get down here for an evening with a knight in shining armor who rode into my diner on the way to slay the dragons of discontent—so what happened at Graceland to turn you into this other person I am not so familiar with?"

Tully finished his drink, and the waiter brought huge brisket sandwiches on hot French bread and horseradish sauce.

"You know, I was feelin' real good about myself when I left home. I quit my job, told Mrs. Barston what I thought of her and her ranch Nazi, and I was on the road. I felt like Charles Kuralt. I had hardly been out of the state of Wyoming, and now I was goin' to see America and the world. Hannibal was not what I expected, but I'm glad I went. But I just wasn't ready for what I found in Graceland." He sighed.

"What did you find?"

"The real meaning of free enterprise," Tully told her. "If it's popular, put it on a T-shirt."

Donna Kay laughed, almost choking on her sandwich. “You are some kind of cowboy philosopher, Tully Mars.”

“Did you ever see *King Creole*?” he asked.

“Of course I did. That movie was one of the reasons I ran away from home and came to New Orleans in the first place.”

“That movie brought new meaning to a dull life in a cow town,” Tully went on. “I grew sideburns, ducktails, and I bought the first purple shirt anyone had ever seen in Heartache, Wyoming. I learned to play the guitar. I named my first horse Tupelo, and I used to have ’em play ‘All Shook Up’ when I rode the bull at the rodeo.

“Well, when I went to Graceland, I saw all the lines of people being herded onto tour buses like cattle at the stockyard. I’m not good in lines, so I just hopped over the fence and walked around sort of like I figured Elvis must have done when he wanted to get a little peace in the valley, and then I realized *he was fenced in*. Trapped in his life just like I had been in mine. I guess it’s hard to be a hero. Well, I wandered up to the house, finally, and found the Memorial Garden, and I was reading the writing on Elvis’s grave and cryin’ my eyes out like all the rest of the people when the guards came up and threw me out for jumpin’ the fence.

“Back on the street I saw more buses and lines and T-shirt shops and Elvis-this and Elvis-that and wondered about all those other people who you think have it made but are really locked up—the President, the Pope, Rin Tin Tin. And I was glad to be who I was and know I could go where I wanted to go.”

Donna Kay sat across the table, tears welling up in her eyes. She leaned over and kissed Tully on the lips.

"Let's go dancin'," she said.

Donna Kay met up with her old friends Bridgette and Evelyn, who still lived on Governor Nichols Street. Evelyn managed a hotel on Royal Street called the Cornstalk, and Donna Kay had called earlier and gotten a room. These girls were dancin' fools, and after a few tequilas at the Napoleon House, they took Tully out on the town.

The first stop was Tippatina's where Zachary Richard, the Cajun Mick Jagger, had the girls thinking about mortal sin. He sang in French but danced in a language those southern women all understood. Tully twirled around the dance floor, weaving between Donna Kay, Bridgette, and Evelyn. The night wore on.

They stopped at the Camellia Grill for a cheeseburger and then finished the night off at Storyville where Luther Kent growled out the blues, and they slow-danced until the sun came up. Donna Kay and Tully walked back to the hotel arm in arm and passed the St. Louis Cathedral; the faithful were filing in for seven o'clock mass.

They slept all day and made love in the canopy bed behind thick purple curtains that separated them from the light and noise in the street. Tully woke up out of sync with time and place, and he was alone except for the fragrance of Donna Kay's perfumed note pinned to the pillow.

Tully,

Thank you for a wonderful excuse to get the hell out of Dodge. Bridgette and Evelyn told me to tell you that you didn't dance bad for a white boy. I was never very good at keeping a man probably because I wound up smothering them, so I am on my way back to the simple life I have chose for myself, but it sure as hell was fun to kick up my heels. Just remember that you cannot change the world or the cruel and heartless way it seems to spin at times, just be thankful that you have the notion to "light out into the territory" as that white-haired old philosopher of yours used to say. You have a wonderful spirit and trust your heart to lead you where you want to go. I have never been to the Caribbean and do like horses. You have the number and it won't be changing anytime soon. Call me if you want some company.

Love,

Donna Kay

Tully walked down to the edge of the Mississippi, near the old brewery. He watched the tugs pushing big freighters toward the middle of the river where they picked up steam and disappeared around the bend. A log was drifting past, close to shore, and he stared at it long and hard.

"Holy shit," he blurted out. Tully could not believe his eyes, for there, perched on the log was the frog he had met up with in Hannibal.

"Well, howdy, Mr. Frog!" Tully shouted as he scrambled down the rocks toward the river's edge.

He was about to scoop up the frog but stopped. The frog had his own places to go, and he had certainly made it this far without any help from some meddling human. So Tully just waved and said "adios" as the log passed on by. The frog stared at Tully and let out a big "rrribit."

Tully Mars picked up Mr. Twain and drove out of town on the old road. He stayed on Highway 90 so he could smell and feel the salt air as he headed east along the Mississippi coast. He wanted to call Donna Kay, but he didn't know what to say. At the Alabama-Mississippi state line, he spotted a big, new, red, double-axle Chevy pickup with a giant aluminum horse trailer attached. It was parked in front of a hamburger stand. He heard Mr. Twain whinny, and Tully's old truck seemed to steer itself into the lot. A tall man wearing what Tully knew as a horseshow-prize silver buckle walked out of the hamburger stand toward the shiny rig. He was eating a chili cheese dog.

MARCH 25, 1989

It is a long way from Heartache, Wyoming to Grand Bay, Alabama, the watermelon capital of the world, but I made it. There ain't many watermelons around yet, but there sure are a lot of cutting horses, something I didn't expect to see in Alabama. Mr. Twain is happier than a pig in shit and I have ridden him every day since I got here. But I'm getting ahead of myself. I met this fellow the other day when I stopped for a chili dog. His name's Clark Gable, just like the movie star. But this Clark Gable is a cutting horse trainer who lives down here in Alabama. He and I hit it off right away when he saw my Wyoming plates. He has traveled all over the West trading horses and has a beautiful little ranch down here where he works cattle for some big rancher down in Florida and to beat everything, he's just thirty minutes from the beach. Today I am going to see the ocean for the first time and I am more excited than I can remember. Clark's ranch is named the Gulf and Western and he has a mural of a school of mermaids watching this cowboy riding a giant bucking shrimp painted on the roof of his barn. I must say this is the kind of place I could surely get used to. The weather has been incredible since I hit Alabama and people are gladly saying good-bye to winter and hello to spring. Clark told me that they had a pretty bad winter and that it got down to twenty a couple of times. I told him that it hadn't gotten above twenty back in Heartache for a month before I left. It is already hot here and I just layed out all day yesterday trying to get a little sun. Clark saw me spread-eagle in the grass and commented that he hadn't seen that much white meat since Thanksgiving. He is a great guy and just took me in like I was his long lost brother or something. I have been helping him around here since right off the bat, and he is thankful to have someone who knows about horses like I do cause like everywhere else these days, good help is hard to find. I don't know how long I plan to stay cause I want to get down to that island soon. Clark has already told me that he would love for me to stay and work for him but he understood my wanderlust because he had gone to sea as a young man. I had to ask him what that meant and when I found out, I'm glad I've got it.

Clark has a friend who runs a shrimp boat over in a little place called Heat Wave on the island of Snake Bite Key and he said that he would talk to him for me about working my way south on a boat. I told him that I had to take Mr. Twain along and he understood and thought that his friend would understand. Talked to Donna Kay the other night and things are fine in Blytheville but I do get confusing feelings about this woman because she is not like any woman I have met before. She seems to understand what I am trying to do better than I do which makes it hard for me to understand just what the hell I am doing. Anyway, today is a beautiful spring day and the dogwoods and azaleas have turned this place pink and white all over and we are headed for the beach.

T.M.
Grand Bay, Alabama

Clark drove Tully to the western tip of Dauphin Island, one of the barrier islands that stretch from the mouth of the Mississippi River to the foot of Florida. Surf fishermen stood waist-deep in the water, casting into the outgoing tide for speckled trout. They gave Clark and Tully some odd looks as the horses were unloaded.

Sonny, one of the hired hands, took the trailer to the other end of the island where he would meet them later. Clark knew one of the fishermen and stayed to chat awhile.

"Tully, you go on ahead," he said. He knew this was a pretty special moment for his friend and let him be.

A strong wind blew out of the southwest, and sand

dunes shimmered in the distance. Tully, bare chested and barefoot, was seated on Mr. Twain's bare back. To Tully's surprise, Mr. Twain had no fear of the water or birds or noise of the surf. First they galloped, walked, and trotted down the beach, and then Tully sent Mr. Twain head-on into the waves. The force of the water knocked them back toward the beach. Tully held on tight to Mr. Twain's mane—it suddenly dawned on him that he didn't know how to swim.

Mr. Twain made a wide circle and then swam for shore. Helped along by a cresting wave, horse and rider bodysurfed into the shallow water. As Mr. Twain rolled on the beach, Tully spotted a school of dolphins playing nearby. They came right up to the shoreline and checked out the big brown animal and the small red-and-white man.

Tully stuck his nose out as far as it would go and was breathing in the salt air. Fiddler crabs and sea gulls scurried out of the way as the Gulf let go all of its energy. Then gravity pulled it back. The next wave came in like clockwork. Tully had been watching the motion of the ocean for a solid hour before Clark finally caught up with him and Mr. Twain where the paved road began.

"You made it, cowboy," Clark said, riding up alongside. A string of fish was looped around his saddle horn.

"I feel like fuckin' Lawrence of Arabia!"

"I know," Clark sighed. "I never get tired of this view."

The two men rode together down past the new beach houses that had been rebuilt after the last hurricane. Tully looked out over the Gulf of Mexico and imagined what was on the other side of the water. He saw himself on Mr. Twain, riding the beaches of the Caribbean. He would be like the Spaniards who had first brought horses to the New World. Then he and Mr. Twain would ride together down the chain of smaller islands that stretched all the way to the Amazon River.

"I want to see it all," Tully told Clark.

"I know the feelin', son."

They met up with Sonny near the ferry dock. After washing the salt off the horses and themselves, they cooked the speckled trout on a grill and devoured them with lots of hot sauce and cold beer. Clark went over to the docks and brought back a sack of fresh oysters. They polished them off for dessert and then drove back to the ranch.

That night Tully reread *Following the Equator* and decided if he didn't move out soon, he might never leave.

The next morning, Clark drove him down to Dauphin Island. Tully was leaving his trusty truck and trailer with Clark and would ride on the beach, heading toward Heat Wave. He saddled Mr. Twain. He planned to look up Clark's shrimper friend and try to go south.

"I'll drop you a postcard when I get to where I'm goin'," Tully said.

"I'll watch out for your truck. And if the jungle gets too lonely, you know what the Mexicans say: 'Mi casa, su casa,' " Clark told him.

He and Tully sat on a picnic bench under an oak tree near Fort Gaines to wait for the ferry. People fished on nearby pilings, and Tully wished he had time to take out his fly rod and join them. But there would be plenty of time for fishing where he was going.

He looked out over the old Civil War fort toward a lighthouse on a distant little sandspit at the mouth of Mobile Bay.

"I just love the idea that I could get on a boat right here and head out there for anywhere in the world. It's pretty overpowering," Tully remarked.

Clark laughed. "Not to everybody. I had this guy who worked for me run away from Detroit with a seventeen-year-old babysitter because she wanted to see the ocean. Bad case of middle-aged man lettin' the little head think for the big head. He was a pretty successful doctor up North, but he left his family, his practice, his whole life to take his midwestern Lolita to the beach.

"So he drove nonstop all the way from Michigan to Panama City, Florida, and he took the babysitter by the hand and led her up to a sand dune so she could finally look out over the ocean. She stared for quite a while and then turned to the man and said, 'Gee, Dr. Bob, I thought it would be bigger.' "

The ferryboat docked, and Tully rode Mr. Twain on board to the delight of some small children playing nearby in the shallow water. As he and his horse crossed Mobile Bay on the ferry, Tully talked to an old man in a pickup who told him about the war years, when German U-boats hovered off Sand Island and picked off freighters setting out to sea.

He pointed northeast and said to Tully, "Up there, the Coast Guard boys actually sunk a U-boat, and I heard tell that some of the bodies of them Nazi sailors washed ashore, and they found used ticket stubs from the Saenger Theater in New Orleans in their pockets. I bet you never heard that before, have ya?"

Tully smiled, "No, I sure haven't."

APRIL 1, 1989

I am shipping out, and this ain't no April Fool's joke. It happened so fast I can't believe it, but it is happening and I can't sleep at all, but just stare out from this little house on Bar-B-Q Hill at the moon on the ocean. I am on the island of Snake Bite Key and it feels like a dream. I rode across the entire Alabama coastline barefoot. I had never spent that much time in my life out of a pair of boots and my toes truly enjoyed their new found freedom but my heels are now covered with Band-Aids. The rangers at Fort Morgan gave me permission to ride the beach through the state park and we were joined by a couple of golden retrievers who came out of the sand dunes and traveled with us till we got to Gulf Shores. I had never seen tall buildings on the beach before and think that they look like they belong somewhere else. I tell you it seems like a million years ago when I left Wyoming and I have no desire to return. I rode across the Perdido Bay Bridge and stopped Mr. Twain on the Florida-Alabama border so that half of him could be in one state while the other half was in another state at the same time.

Had lunch at a place called the Flora-Bama and ate more oysters and discovered fried crab claws. I love em, cause they taste like the ocean. The bartender at the Flora-Bama was originally from Hardin, Montana, and we talked about the battlefield and he sort of got confused about how I got down here and told everybody that I had ridden my horse all the way which got all the people in the place interested in what kind of animal could make the trip and went out to check out Mr. Twain who seemed to handle fame quite well. The bartender told me that they had a great band that night but I told him I had to get to Heat Wave. He wouldn't let me pay for the beer and oysters and bought me a Florida lottery ticket as a going away present for good luck. And he let me keep Mr. Twain outside behind the bar. People who live on the beach seem to live at a slower, friendlier pace and it is something I could get real used to real fast.

When I got off the ferry boat in Heat Wave I called Clark's friend, Captain Kirk Patterson, and he said he had been hoping to hear from me because if I was serious about heading south, he was leaving the next day for Key West on his shrimp boat and they had room for Mr. Twain. There was a terrible rainstorm last night, so I waited until early this morning to ride up here from the beach. I crossed the causeway and stopped for a minute and watched this funny-looking man make a hole in one on the golf course. Kirk met me at the bridge. He was a lot younger than I expected. I guess I figured all boat captains look like Long John Silver. He told me that the weather had delayed their departure for a day but I was still welcome to make the trip if I would be willing to cook and lend a hand on deck. We went to a little place called the Northern Lights Cafe where I met these two crazy sisters named Aurora and Bora Alice who owned the place. They called her Boring Alice, but she was anything but that. Kirk told me that one of them was now the football coach at the local high school. We chatted for a while and I told them that I had waited all my life until I could see the ocean before I ate seafood. I told them the story about the guy from Jackson Hole and they busted a gut laughing and then proceeded to fix me the most incredible seafood platter in the world. Shrimps, crabs, oysters, flounder, hushpuppies, West Indies Salad, cole slaw, and tartar sauce. When I finished eating, they asked if I was staying long cause if I was the fresh fish supply in the Gulf could be in danger of disappearing. Boy, was that good chow.

We walked around town and they were sort of like tour guides and gave me a little history of the place which was great for I had never thought about Alabama as being on the ocean. Last night we all went to a little beach bar called the Homeport. Kirk's brother, who is a famous piano player that I had never heard of named Slade Patterson was on the island visiting his family and we had a little jam session which lasted until well into the morning. He was really a nice guy and he has been all around the world, but still tries to come home whenever he can. I felt a little sad, when I saw how strongly these folks were tied to their island and I hope that one day, I will have a place that I can call home too. Well enough of that piss and moan shit. We had a great bon voyage party as Slade called it and I can see the sky beginning to turn pink in the east and I must confess, I could use some rest for tomorrow I go out on the big bad ocean. Ain't life grand.

T.M.
Heat Wave, Alabama

Tully rode Mr. Twain through the sand streets of Heat Wave down to the shrimp docks, where several boats were preparing to leave. He tied Mr. Twain to a crab trap. The boat he was looking for was at the end of the pier.

The waterfront had its own smell—something between essence of shrimp and diesel fuel. Captain Kirk and his crew were loading the huge net onto the *Caribbean Soul*, an enormous white boat with a high bow and two big towers behind the wheelhouse. It may have been a shrimp boat, but it looked like the *Queen Mary* to the cowboy from Heartache.

"A man who is on time. I like that," Kirk called out when he saw Tully.

"Can I give you a hand?"

"Climb on up here, cowboy. You can start by loading those provisions down into the galley."

"And exactly where would that be?"

"That would be what you used to call a kitchen before you stepped on this vessel." Kirk laughed. "Spud, Willy, this here is Tully Mars, and he and his trusted horse will be going with us to Key West."

A carrot-topped young man covered with tattoos waved from atop the tower, and the black man on deck extended his hand across the dock. "I'm Spud, and he's Willy," he said. "How's your cookin', cowboy?"

"I been eatin' it for twenty years, and it hasn't killed me yet."

"Well, welcome aboard," Spud said.

"Not so fast there," Kirk shouted as he made his way across the boat. He went into the wheelhouse and came out with a pair of white rubber boots.

"Put these on. You could bust your ass in those shit kickers you're wearin'," he said. Tully put his prize pair of Tony Lama's into the duffel bag and slipped into the rubber boots. He was now a shrimper.

That morning they loaded the big net on board, checked the rigging, and fueled the boat. Once underway Tully would cook and lend a hand on deck, doing whatever Spud and Willy told him to do. Just before noon the boat was ready to go, and Kirk gave the crew an hour to take care of whatever they needed to before leaving. Mr. Twain would be loaded last.

Kirk said the weather looked real good for the trip to Key West. It would take about two and a half days, and they shouldn't have any problems with the horse being on deck.

In the last-minute rush, Tully called Donna Kay at the Chat 'n Chew, but the girl who answered the phone said it was Donna Kay's day off from work, and she had gone to Memphis. Tully then called Clark to thank him for his help, scribbled a postcard to Joe McCormick, and went to the Northern Lights Cafe for a cheeseburger.

A little after one o'clock, Tully cautiously led Mr. Twain aboard the *Caribbean Soul*. They stood together on the bow as Kirk steered the big boat down Little Billy Creek toward the Perdido Bay Bridge and the open sea.

Someone called his name as they passed under the bridge, and he broke out of his daydream to see Aurora and Bora Alice at the breakwater taking pictures of the cowboy and his horse on the bow of a boat.

"You look great!" Aurora yelled out.

"I feel great!" Tully yelled back.

Tully let the ocean breeze caress him until they passed the farewell buoy and the slow, steady rolling waves began to move the boat up and down. He led Mr. Twain to a little roped-off section near the stern and tied him up. Mr. Twain seemed perfectly happy. Tully sat beside him on a coiled stack of line and watched the land disappear slowly behind them. He felt a rush of goose bumps and let out a big sigh. He patted Mr. Twain on the neck.

Tully Mars had kept his promise to his faithful horse and had brought him to the shore, and now beyond. Adventure, he hoped, lay ahead, and he had surely left some unfinished business behind—always a good excuse to return.

APRIL 4, 1989

I didn't get sick and Willy told me that the storm we ran into off of Tampa was a pretty bad one and I got compliments on my cooking. Mr. Twain held up beautifully all the way and the crew has sort of adopted him as a good luck charm. We crossed the Gulf of Mexico in about two and a half days and got to Key West early this morning. I have been studying Captain Kirk's charts and learning about fathoms and bearings and stuff. I had to take my stand at the watch and didn't want to leave. Steering a big boat like the Caribbean Soul is a lot like riding a horse and as Kirk says, you have to develop a touch. This afternoon we are going to take Mr. Twain out on the beach and I am going to teach the crew how to ride. I don't really understand how I ever spent thirty-nine winters in Wyoming. Willy and Spud told me to cut a pair of my jeans and make shorts so that I could get some sun and look like a native. The island popped up on the horizon just after dawn and looked like the Emerald City. I guess Key West is part of America but it sort of seems like an outpost to me. I mean it just sits right out in the middle of the ocean. The water is incredibly clear and as soon as I learn how to swim, I'm going to take up snorkling.

We tied up the Caribbean Soul at the shrimp docks near town and Spud took Mr. Twain to the park. I went straight to Ernest Hemingway's house to have a look around. No wonder he wrote such good books living in those kinds of surroundings. Kirk is just icing-up here and he told me that I was welcome to stay on board to Campeche and I had a job if I wanted one. It's just a hop, skip, and a jump across the Gulf from here to the Yucatan Peninsula and I really don't have any other plans. I went to the bookstore and bought a book about navigating which I figure I will get some practice on when we cross the Gulf again. I went down to the Sunset Dock where everybody goes to watch the sun drop into the ocean and it was pretty neat that here people take the time to watch one of the prettiest things in the world. Mr. Twain seems to like this warm weather and right now he is staying with a friend of Kirk's who has two horses of his own. Tonight we all went down to Captain Tony's Bar and drank some tequilla and watched a bunch of college girls get drunk and enter the wet T-shirt contest which is as bad as they seem to want to get these days. I am studying my Spanish in my bunk as we head out early in the morning. I am starting with the necessities of life like oysters and beer and heuvos rancheros.

T.M.
Key West, Florida

It was raining hard when the postman rushed through the door of the Chat 'n Chew. He stomped around on the soggy doormat and shook as much of the rain off his parka as he could.

"Thank you very much, Hollis," Donna Kay said. She was stretched out in a corner booth reading a copy of *Islands* magazine. It had rained for eight straight days, which meant flood season was in high gear along the banks of the Mississippi River. She got up and walked slowly to the counter.

"Trade ya your mail for a cup of coffee," Hollis said.

"I thought you were a public servant, but I guess nothin' is really free these days," Donna Kay replied.

She poured Hollis a steaming cup of coffee, and he handed her a bundle of letters. She thumbed through the usual junk mail and then saw the letter from Tully. The envelope had a drawing of a stick man on a stick horse under a palm tree and was covered with brightly colored stamps from some banana republic.

Hollis finished his coffee and shuffled back out into the rain. Donna Kay went back to the booth and opened the letter carefully so as not to tear the pretty stamps. Several photos and a Florida lottery ticket fell out of the bundle of folded yellow pages.

MAY 15, 1989

Dear Donna Kay,

Hello from paradise. The weather is here wish you were beautiful (ha ha). I tried to phone you a bunch of times but we kept missing each other. I know I should have written earlier but things were happening pretty fast. I know that is no excuse, but I hope that you haven't fallen in love and run off with some Arab prince or oil man from Shreveport and that you will still be at the Chat 'n Chew when and if this letter makes it.

Donna Kay looked out the window of the diner. A big eighteen-wheeler roared by in the downpour. She shook her head and wiped her eyes, shook her head again and laughed. "That son of a bitch," she said to nobody and picked up where she had left off.

I enclosed these photos so that you will be able to recognize the new me. The first one is me taken a couple of days ago by my friend Ramon with his Polaroid. I didn't shave on the crossing between Key West and Cozumel but when I finally looked in the mirror, I sort of liked the beard.

The second picture is me at the tattoo parlor with Willy. That's the star system called the Pleiades on my right shoulder. Madame Stella, the voodoo lady who owns the Live Bait and Sushi Bar, told me that it is where the Atlantians came from to settle the earth, and I had lived there in a former life. I told her that I was still trying to figure out which life I am leading in this world. I feel like I have lived about five different lives at the same time since I left Wyoming. First I was back in Custer's cavalry on that battlefield, and then I went to see the birthplace of my hero but wound up wishing I was a frog floating on a log. I had just about figured women were out of my life and was getting into being alone when I met this incredible lady (that's you) who blew all my latest theories to hell. One day I was a cowboy and the next day I was at the wheel of an eighty-foot-boat crossing the Gulf of Mexico, and then one day I was flat broke and happy and the next minute I was rich and didn't care.

Who-a-a-a big fella. I'm getting a little ahead of myself but there is a whole lot to tell so let me back up. I got here on a shrimp boat named the Caribbean Soul from Heat Wave, Alabama, which was owned by Captain Kirk Patterson, who was a good friend of Clark Gable who I met in the watermelon capital of the world where I left my truck. I hope that clears things up a little. I worked on the boat for a couple of weeks and then they went back to Key West but should be returning soon. I decided to stay and practice my Spanish and study celestial navigation so that I could find my way home when the time comes. Nobody here has a real name and nobody talks about former lives. They call me the Spaceman cause Madame Stella says I come from another planet.

I am living on the beach in a hut with a palm thatched roof. My neighbor is an old snake oil salesman from somewhere up in America. They call him the Twelve Volt Man. He is the closest thing they have to a preacher here and every Friday evening he fills up his little Honda generator with gas and fires it up. It is connected to an old Sears Die Hard battery which powers a blender and a tape player. Well, he puts his A1A cassette in and starts that blender whirring and we drink margaritas until the sun drops into the ocean or he runs out of gas, whichever comes first.

The third photo is Mr. Twain, yes can you believe it, he is now a palomino and get this, he is in love with this little filly owned by the lady who runs the bakery/space station. His mane started turning blond on the boat and I figured it to be a sure sign that the change in latitude was agreeing with him. The kids riding him were my guides at the Mayan ruins at Tulum. I rode up there one day and found the place swarming with American tourists, but these kids singled me out since I was the only person who had come by horse and told me to wait until the buses went back to Cancun and then they took me through the ruins as the full moon came up. It was pretty wild out there, I tell you.

The fourth photo is me and my buddy Whale in the bar at the Island Hotel with the winning ticket. I went into town to have a beer and get some stamps and I stopped by the bar where a lot of expatriated Americans hang out and watch the Cubs games and porno flicks on the satellite dish. Anyway I was paying for my beer when this lottery ticket that somebody gave me up in Alabama fell out of my pocket and Whale picked it up and gave it to me. He is from Ft. Myers, Florida, and told me all about the big bucks lottery. I had forgotten all about it, but when I scraped the ink off I'll be darned if I didn't win $10,000.00 which gets us to the point of this letter. If you can break away from the Chat 'n Chew for a few days, I would like you to do me a favor and call my friend Kirk Patterson in Heat Wave. He knows all about you, or at least as much as I know about you, and cash in this ticket and buy yourself a first class air fare to Belize City and bring me the change. Kirk can get in touch with me on the Coconut Telegraph and I will meet you there. I really hope you can come and I know it is a lot to ask but this place is something you have got to see and we have a lot of catching up to do. Donna Kay, all my life I have dreamed about a place like this. When I was a little kid I used to dream about this island that was so beautiful and inhabited by the friendliest people I could ever imagine but it has no name and was always changing oceans on me. I could never quite figure out where it was, but I kept having that dream again and again and would look forward to it when it popped into my head, and then one day, I knew it was time to dream no more but to find out what was out there for me in the real world, and that is why I was afraid to stay in New Orleans or go back up to see you though I thought about it often. I had to see this thing through. If I had stopped in New Orleans or Grand Bay, or Heat Wave, it would have been like Columbus not going any farther west than the first island he came to when he set out to discover an entire New World. Hell, he thought Cuba was China and never made it to where he was going. I hope you can make some sense out of all of this and even if you can't I hope your gypsy soul that got you to New Orleans will lead you here. My daddy used to say that in a hundred years, none of this will matter, but right now it does. I miss you. Donna Kay Dunbar, come on dowwwwwn

Love,

Tully-The Spaceman
Wasting Away in Margaritaville

OFF TO SEE THE LIZARD

Aurora and Bora Alice Porter stood outside the Northern Lights Cafe and admired the freshly painted window. Across the glass in huge purple-and-white letters was written "Lick 'Em Lizards." Football season was two weeks from opening, and though the rest of Heat Wave hardly gave it a thought, this was an important day for the Porter girls, for they had succeeded in getting the coach they wanted.

Romeo Fleming was the topic of conversation among the breakfast boys seated around the biggest table in the cafe. He had taken the job as interim head coach of the Heat Wave High Lizards after the last coach, Sid Wickstraw, had resigned for "health reasons" and entered the Trappist monastery.

"What the hell kind of name is Romeo for a football coach anyway?" Jasper Jetters asked.

"Well, it fits right in with the program, I'd say," Vince Patterson smirked. "We now have the only integrated team in the state with an 0–10–1 record and a part-time English teacher named Romeo as the new head coach."

"Seems to me we'll be the laughingstock of the state again," J. B. Docker muttered.

Aurora Porter winked at her identical twin sister as she flipped blueberry pancakes on the griddle and looked out the window. A shrimp boat was arriving, and she waved at it. "Romeo Fleming was a badass linebacker for the New York Giants, and damn near as cute as Frank Gifford," she said.

Boring Alice, as the locals affectionately nicknamed her, chimed in, "But I really liked the articles he used to write for *Life*." She poured coffee for the men seated around the big table. It was the girls who had convinced Romeo to take the job.

"Well, I never heard of him bein' no pro ballplayer," Jasper said without looking up from his copy of the *National Fisherman*.

"He was the best linebacker in the state of Florida. He's from Milton, but he played college ball at Notre Dame," Aurora said.

Silence filled the Northern Lights for a moment. In unison, the men at the big table uttered the words again in disgust, "Notre Dame."

Aurora and Boring Alice Porter had come to Heat Wave with their archaeologist father. He was in search of the remains of prehistoric sea monsters that used to inhabit the bogs of Snake Bite Key back when the world was one big seafood stew, and humans were just another catch of the day.

When Dr. Porter unearthed the first fossil skeleton,

the newly built high school adopted the lizard as its mascot. Dr. Porter coached the team during its glory years, but that was long ago. Aurora and Boring Alice had grown up in the grandstands. But then they moved away to Nepal when their father went looking for more history.

After he died, they returned to Heat Wave and opened the cafe. They were still ardent supporters of the Lizards and never missed a game.

In this part of the world football was like religion. The big schools from the big towns went about it with the blind-faith fervor of the Spanish Inquisition. Overbearing fathers prolonged their youth through the limber limbs of their offspring, screaming for their teams to tear the fucking head off every opponent. The carnage culminated when their sons were chosen to walk the hallowed road to Tuscaloosa and play for Bear Bryant, who, to these folks, was more important than God.

But Snake Bite Key had always been a place unto itself since the days it was discovered and populated by the French Canadian explorer Iberville. People there moved to a different drum. Twenty miles north of Highway 90 put you in redneck country where they referred to the inhabitants of Snake Bite Key as "bay rat spooks and nigger lovers." In Heat Wave, football had to share the stage with other human concerns: fishing, dancing, singing, and going to the beach. Besides, there were only twenty-five male students in the high school.

The isolation of the island produced a natural integration of blacks and whites. There was one church, one school, and one island; the joy and pain of life in a fishing village was shared equally by everyone. Most people cared little for the rest of the state anyway and still considered Snake Bite Key part of Louisiana, as Thomas Jefferson had originally planned it. They raised their families from the bounty of the sea and enjoyed the pleasures of island living—which had nothing to do with most of the rest of Alabama. The ambivalent attitude toward football was deep-seated in local tradition—with the exception of Aurora and Boring Alice Porter.

Romeo Fleming took all these things into consideration as he pulled his little skiff up to his dock. He unloaded two speckled trout and dropped them into the live well where they would stay until they were needed. He still didn't know why he had taken the job, but as Boring Alice had put it, "Even the quiet and calm places of the world have to be shaken up every now and then just to keep life interesting." This seemed to be one of those times.

Romeo thought the owners of the Northern Lights Cafe were two of the most knowledgeable but crazy women he had ever encountered. They were the only people on the island who knew of his past as both a football player and a journalist, and they were always interesting company. He had been eating a cheeseburger in the cafe when the girls had started up a conversation about how grand it would be—just once—to field a winning team; now, with the departure of Coach Wickstraw, the aperture to greatness was finally open. They talked of Romeo's glory days as a player, and after several beers he left the cafe and went right to the principal's office and volunteered to be the coach for the rest of the year.

The girls had told him it was his destiny to coach the

team—as the vociferous Aurora had put it, "You know, Romeo, you just don't fuck with fate."

He had grown up in the small Panhandle town of Milton, the son of an English teacher. He escaped by being an all-American linebacker for the fighting Irish, which had thrown him on the merry-go-round of life, spinning him from South Bend, Indiana, around the world God knows how many times—and now, ironically, back to within sixty miles of where he had started out. Just as ironic, he had also ended up being what he had wanted to be when he left home so many years ago: a writer of fiction living on the beach.

In his former lives he had been married to a stewardess, had been an all-pro linebacker with the Giants, and had worked in New York for a big newspaper. As a correspondent, his travels across the world constantly opened new cans of strange encounters—from dancing with Imelda Marcos in the Philippines to living with the Vietcong to narrowly escaping death when an ammunition ship he was aboard blew up and shot him into the Pacific sky like a Roman candle. The ship sank, but he survived and spent two months adrift in a lifeboat and three months on an island inhabited only by iguanas. His documentation of the whole ordeal was published and made the best-seller list.

Now he was ready for a breather. He had taken a small house west of Heat Wave, was working on a second book, and teaching part-time at the high school for the pleasure of it. His skiff, a duffel bag full of warm-weather clothes, and an old Hallicraft shortwave were his only possessions. He did not consider Hector a pet. Hector, his iguana, was part of his life. He was a charm, a good luck charm Romeo had discovered a long time ago. Hector had shown him the way to a watering hole that had saved his life. They sat up at night together and listened to the hissing broadcasts from around the world on the Hallicraft—which made Romeo thankful he was where he was.

His first meeting with the football team was in the gym on a hot day late in August. He wore a pair of khaki shorts, a Hawaiian shirt, flip-flops, and a pair of reflector sunglasses. He strolled down Main Street with his lizard in tow. When the big iguana got up on his legs and walked, his body stood three feet in the air and presented a frightening view to other members of the animal kingdom, who scurried for shelter.

Romeo walked into the gym, and the smell of sweat, wood, wax, and liniment hit him immediately and re-kindled memories of his own high school days. Across the floor, twenty young men stood talking and shooting lay-ups, but they all stopped dead in their tracks when they saw Romeo and the lizard approaching.

"Be seated, please," Romeo called out.

He walked toward them, past a movie projector and a screen. He stopped in front of the boys, and the big lizard let out a hiss, flicked his tongue twice, and set himself down next to Romeo on the parquet floor. The exhaust fans squeaked overhead.

"Good morning. I am Romeo Fleming. Some of you know me from English literature classes, but from now on you can call me Coach."

He let the silence sit for a moment. When the big reptile flicked his green tongue at the team, some of them moved farther up in the bleachers. Young faces looked at each other wondering where the hell this guy came from.

"This is Hector—your new mascot. I was in a tight spot once, and he was the only friend I had. He is a good luck charm. In the ancient civilizations and mythologies of the world the lizard is a symbol of luck and power. In Australia, they are gods. In Heat Wave, we are only looking for a winning season. We will play football and enjoy it. It is not a matter of life and death.

"I realize you guys take a lot of shit from people for just being in Heat Wave. I never planned to be here either, but fate has ruled. Now we can do one of two things: go through the motions of calling ourselves a football team and do what everybody expects—which is lose most of the time—or we can move together, become a team, win a few games, and have some fun.

"I can tell already that some of you are better players than others. That's just life. But we'll combine all of our talents for the best of the team. Now, back in the stone ages, when I was a player, I was blessed with ability. It got me the glamor of a big-time college stadium filled with a hundred thousand people, the advances of hard-bodied cheerleaders, and the opportunity to play for a professional football team and go to the big city, buy a big car, and have a beautiful girlfriend. In return, I had my body beaten to pulp for a fraction of the money made by the people who owned the team."

Romeo walked up to the first row. Hector followed him and faced the team.

"This year, we are going to be kick-some-ass Lizards. Any questions?"

Billy Purdy, the quarterback and captain, raised his hand. He stood up slowly and pointed at Hector. "Aren't iguanas vegetarians?" he asked.

Romeo grinned. "Yeah, but the other team doesn't have to know that. Now, we don't have much time, so let's get to work." He turned out the lights and turned on the movie projector.

"Today we are going to study a game film," Romeo said. He sat down in the bleachers with his team as *Godzilla* came on the screen. From the back of the gymnasium, Aurora and Boring Alice watched the movie.

"He's gonna do just fine," Alice said. She shoved her hand into the bag of popcorn her sister held.

It was another sweltering day when Aurora and Boring Alice walked to the cafe.

"I think it's great that he made Godzilla the new mascot. This is a new attitude," Aurora said.

"Godzilla was a misunderstood individual," Boring Alice added. "It seems only right he should be the mascot."

They moved into the sanctuary of the air-conditioned cafe. Aurora flicked on the lights and started the coffee machine while Boring Alice filled the syrup pitchers. "Do you remember when we lived in Australia, and Papa took us to Ayer's Rock?" Alice asked. "Where we camped in the Valley of the Moon in the Land of Linga the Lizard Man?"

"Oh yes. Déjà, déjà, déjà vu," Aurora sang, and Boring Alice joined in. This was the song their father taught them when they lived in Australia.

"It pisses me off when I hear those old farts puttin' down the Lizards for lack of anything better to do. It does seem strange that the team only has ten plays, though," Aurora said.

Boring Alice rubbed a little Pledge on the old jukebox. ''Remember that great gift the Gecko Woman gave Papa?'' she asked. ''It was my seventh birthday, and she sang to me about the Goanna men who hoarded the water, and how the Gecko Woman tricked them and gave the water to the rest of the world. She gave Papa her magic lizard skin costume.''

''Earth to Alice, come in. I switched the topic of conversation to football. Try to stay in the game, honey. Here comes the coach.''

Aurora fussed with her hair, and Alice put a quarter in the jukebox and played Benny Spellman's ''Fortune Teller,'' ''Mule Train'' by Frankie Laine, and ''Purple People Eater.'' Aurora danced to the door and flipped over the Open sign just as Romeo Fleming came in.

''Good morning, Coach,'' Alice said. ''How's practice going with the Godzillas?''

''Great name,'' Aurora added. She was still dancing around the floor.

''Fine. Aurora, what do you know about the Bundy team?'' Romeo asked.

''Big, mean redneck boys. Their life's ambition is to get a job at the Pulptown paper mill. Rather unimaginative offense, and they play dirty. They won the state championship last year,'' Aurora told him.

''I know. I guess they figure we're cannon fodder for the opener.''

''No doubt about it. They've got this quarterback named Glenn Tidwell—a six-foot-seven, twenty-two-year-old sophomore, married with two kids. He's actually rumored to be around twenty-five, and he throws the ball farther than he can add. You want something to eat, Coach?'' Aurora asked.

"I think it's wonderful how you're pursuing the spiritual side of a contact sport and instilling the power of our ancestral beasts into these present-day warriors by choosing Godzilla as a mascot. But I can't decide whether I really admire you for that or dislike you for abandoning your career as a writer—for the pursuit of gridiron glory," Alice said. She dusted off another table.

"Could I get a cup of coffee and some cinnamon toast, please?" Romeo asked.

"Alice, indecision may or may not be your problem," Aurora snorted and laughed.

"Deep down where it counts, my sister is very shallow," Boring Alice retorted. A flurry of verbal jabs were exchanged like boxers in a clinch.

The breakfast boys methodically shuffled toward the cafe as Aurora and Boring Alice lovingly continued to trade insults. It was an old habit.

"Where fort art dow, Coach?" old man Purdy snickered.

"Off to see the Lizard," Romeo answered.

In most places, September meant fall was in the air, but in Heat Wave it was just another long, hot month on the way to January. That's when it would finally cool off, and the humidity would let up. The first game was a week away, and things were looking good as Romeo watched his team work out. The heat was almost unbearable until twilight, so that's when Romeo and the Lizards practiced.

His team had dwindled to eighteen players, which meant that a lot of them would be playing both offense and defense. Romeo had taken Aurora's suggestion that they practice in the sand on the beach. It had been one of her father's little tricks. Everybody wore high-top black shoes and plodded through the sand.

He had worked out a variation of the old winged-T offense and had moved his most promising player, a solid young black man named Willett Rainer Snow, to tailback. Billy Purdy was a good quarterback, and Eugene Rawls was a pretty quick little wide receiver. He was called "Balls" by his teammates—a tribute to his tenacity.

The Lizards ran their ten plays again and again in the sands of Snake Bite Key until the moves and formations became fluid. On defense, Romeo's standouts at the end positions were the Beckham brothers, sons of Henry Beckham, the oyster man. Romeo called them his Land Sharks and let them cut their hair into the shapes of fins, and they splattered their helmets and jerseys with shark blood.

Leroy Lessons was his middle linebacker, and his teammates called him "Dr. Boom." He worked every summer for the service station and drew crowds whenever he lifted the engine out of a car and hung it on the block and tackle.

Aurora and Boring Alice watched the practice with binoculars from up on Bar-B-Q Hill.

"Can you imagine how fast they're gonna be on a real field?" Aurora asked.

"This'll be goddamn exciting," Boring Alice said, "but I still think we need some help from the other side."

That evening, after Aurora went to bed, Boring Alice lay on the living room floor of her father's house and followed the slow movement of the ceiling fan blades above her. She hypnotized herself, rewinding the videotape of her life back to that birthday near Ayer's Rock and then slowly wound it forward, until she found what she was looking for.

Romeo Fleming was also up, walking the beach with Hector. Together they plodded along in the breaking surf. He hadn't been able to sleep, but he liked the restlessness he was feeling. It was the day before the battle, and he felt he had prepared as well as he could. His young team had responded to his unorthodox methods, and he hoped he had instilled in them the idea that they could win. He felt no fear—just purpose, like the big lizard that walked ahead of him. The magic of the lizard seemed to be at work in Heat Wave.

Friday morning of the big game the breakfast boys stood at the Northern Lights Cafe in the first waiting line ever. They were looking in at a huge watercolor mural of Godzilla wearing a Heat Wave High jersey. He stood knee deep in the Mobile River, blowing his nuclear halitosis toward the paper mill and the Bundy team. In the background, a pack of charred wolves ran for the hills.

"First we got Romeo, and now we got Aurora and Aliceangelo," J. B. Docker said.

"I ain't never waited in line to eat breakfast in my life," Mr. Purdy grumbled.

Inside the cafe, Aurora and Boring Alice were serving breakfast to the team. Romeo Fleming and Hector were seated near the window, and the big lizard turned to the faces peering through the window and flicked his tongue. The breakfast boys backed farther out into the street.

The coach and the team were in good spirits and

eating heartily. Aurora and Boring Alice were as upbeat as ever, making sure the team was well fed. "Purple People Eater" was playing on the jukebox.

"I'd like to hear a big hand for these ladies who saved us from the school cafeteria today," Romeo yelled out, and a big cheer came up from the Lizards.

"If you guys can kick Bundy's ass, you can eat here every day!" Aurora hollered. She walked over to Romeo Fleming and said, "Alice and I need to talk to you about something in private." They all went into the kitchen.

"I was up most of the night helping Alice paint the mural, and as I was putting the finishing touches on Godzilla, I had a vision or a flashback or something. Anyway, I remembered the secret weapon my father used." Aurora looked around the kitchen to make sure no one was listening and then whispered into Romeo's ear. He started to chuckle and then broke into a roar.

"All's fair in love and war, and this is war. It's wonderful."

Romeo kissed both of them on the cheek and went back into the cafe still laughing. He headed for the door, and Hector instinctively trailed behind, followed by the rest of the Lizards.

"Thanks again, ladies, for your hospitality."

"It was our pleasure, Coach. See you on the bus," Aurora said. As the last of the boys left, Aurora turned to Alice. "Isn't this the greatest? He loved it. He *loved* it." she said.

"He should," Alice replied.

The breakfast boys had decided to stay outside until Romeo cleared out with the lizard.

"Good morning, Coach. Today's the big day, huh?" Mr. Purdy asked.

"It's a good day to die, gentlemen," the coach answered as he passed them at the door.

"There's a good possibility of that happening in Pulptown," Jasper Jetters mumbled under his breath. "I'm starving. Let's eat, if there's anything left." But as they were about to open the door, they heard the lock click, and the Closed sign appeared with a note taped to the bottom. It read: "Off to see the Lizards."

That afternoon, as the bus pulled out for the badlands, the breakfast boys were sitting under the big oak tree playing dominoes. They watched the team's exodus and waved to Boring Alice, who was driving the bus.

"It was nice knowing them," old man Purdy said.

"I have a feeling this could be the last year for football in Heat Wave," J. B. Docker added.

"Then we could get some decent service at the goddamn restaurant," Purdy grumbled.

Aurora had spent all afternoon working on her secret weapon while Alice had been up in the attic tearing through mountains of artifacts. Boring Alice had told Aurora of her trip to the past and what she had discovered.

Boring Alice shifted gears, and her armful of good luck bracelets rattled loudly above the engine noise. Uncharacteristically quiet, Aurora sat in the seat behind her. They listened to the radio and headed inland through the potato fields of Baldwin County.

They were on the causeway across Mobile Bay when it started to rain heavily. Romeo Fleming looked up from his copy of *Winds from the Carolinas* and said, "This is good, this is real good. Lizards like mud."

"How much farther?" Aurora asked.

"I can smell it. Not far now," Boring Alice answered.

They crossed the Cochran Bridge into Pulptown, and the air was tainted with the putrid smell of the local paper mill. The sprawling plant was lit up for the night shift. Alice turned to the team sitting quietly in the bus and yelled, "It's good to see this so you know what you're *not* missing."

The rain continued to fall steadily, but the crowd entering Bundy Stadium didn't seem to feel it. They packed the stands and sat under umbrellas and sheets of plastic waiting for the slaughter to begin. The home field side sported a brand-new concrete grandstand with three giant flag poles. Today they had raised the American flag, the Confederate flag, and a massive green flag bearing a salivating wolf and the words, "Bundy Wolves State Champs 1963."

Across from the new stands stood wooden bleachers reserved for the visiting fans and a vintage World War II Quonset hut, which was more of a storage room than a dressing room. Not one soul sat in the stands when Boring Alice drove the bus up and the team unloaded.

At the corner of the end zone a crowd of white punks gathered to look at the black players and yell insults at them, but Willett and his teammates kept their cool.

"Don't pay any attention to those assholes," Romeo told his team. He casually dropped the leash and said something to Hector, who rushed to the fence and scattered the crowd.

The Heat Wave Lizards dressed quickly and went out

onto the field and began their warm-up drills, sluggishly dropping passes and fumbling hand-offs, just as Romeo Fleming had told them to do. He stood in the foul-weather jacket and watched the practice. At the other end of the field, the Bundy Wolves were lined up for calisthenics, all eighty-five of them. Glenn Tidwell, the star quarterback, stood high above the rest of the team and seemed to be snickering and joking as he pointed toward the eighteen Lizards from Heat Wave.

"I've got his number," Dr. Boom said coldly to the Beckham brothers.

The Bundy band marched out onto the soggy field and played the national anthem. At the end of the song someone in the stands shouted "Get them niggers," which seemed to amuse the crowd.

"Fear not, boys!" Aurora yelled above the noise. "Fear not, for though you may walk in the valley of the shadow of death, you are the meanest sons of bitches in the valley!"

Boring Alice parked the bus in a new spot, sensing that a fast getaway was something to be seriously considered. Then she pulled her bag from the luggage rack and went into the dressing room alone.

The toss of the coin was in progress, and Aurora strolled over to the bench where Romeo and Hector were standing. "Charming place to spend a Friday night, huh? Now I know how the Christians must have felt in the Colosseum!" she yelled to Romeo above the band on the field.

Romeo handed her Hector's leash. "We *could* be in Pittsburgh. Now *that* was a tough stadium. Check out the first play."

Heat Wave had won the toss, and the crowd was on

its feet for the kickoff. The ball sailed through the rainy sky and came down in the hands of Billy Purdy. He followed his blocking to the right, but at the last minute he tossed the ball to Willett Rainer Snow. Snow, meanwhile, had gathered a full head of steam and now churned down the left sideline and was standing in the Bundy end zone while the referees were still looking for the ball in the pileup on the Heat Wave twenty.

The crowd in the stadium was stunned. Billy Purdy kicked the extra point, and Heat Wave led 7–0 with 14:51 left to play in the first quarter.

Aurora was wild with jubilation until she realized that all the eyes in the stadium were on her. The smugness she'd seen on the faces of the Bundy players was now gone. They were mad, and so were the fans. A slow handclap started, and then the crowd rose to their feet, one by one, until everybody was standing and clapping in time as Heat Wave prepared to kick off.

"Where the hell is Alice?" Aurora snarled and bit her lip anxiously.

Billy Purdy kicked the ball high and long. The lone safety for Bundy drifted to the left to position himself for the catch, and at that very moment a sheet of rain plummeted from the heavens. The ball appeared out of the deluge about four feet above the head of the receiver, and he attempted to field the ball. But it arrived at the same time Bill and Bobby Beckham did, and the impact of the collision made the entire crowd gasp. The Land Sharks had attacked.

The runner hit the ground and skidded all the way to the end zone on his butt, trailing a rooster tail. The wet ball came to rest on the Bundy four-yard line and was recovered by Balls Rawls.

The rain had let up now. On the Heat Wave sideline near the point of the play stood Boring Alice in the Gecko Woman's costume, which she had dug out of her father's attic. She was covered in a fire red lizard skin and wore a headdress of feathers, bones, and tusks. She was moving in circles and whooping in some strange dialect.

"My God. It's the bride of Godzilla," Aurora said. Her sister was coming her way.

"How did you like my rain dance?" Alice asked in a muffled voice from inside the huge head.

"Whatever you're doing, keep it up," Aurora told her. And when Hector saw the Lizard Woman, he perked up and began hissing and prancing back and forth on the sidelines.

On the playing field the Lizards broke the huddle and ran a power sweep to the left with Willett Rainer Snow carrying the ball. He fought his way to the two-yard line with eight rednecks on his back, punching, cursing, and kicking. As he hit the ground under the pile, a huge hand came through his face mask trying to gouge his eyes. He got a good lock on the index finger with his teeth and could hear a scream from somewhere in the pile as he bit. His teeth hit bone, and he let go. The referee was unpiling the players.

"That nigger tried to bite my finger off!" the big wounded lineman screamed through a stream of tears.

Willett glared at him. "What's out here is yours." He pointed at his face mask. "But when it comes in *here*, it be mine."

On the next play Billy Purdy faked a hand-off to Willett, kept the ball, and ran the opposite way into the end zone. The extra point kick sailed through the uprights, and Heat Wave led 14–0.

The rains continued to pour down, and soon nobody could tell black players from white players since they were all covered with mud. The Heat Wave defense played with tenacity, and Bundy could not get untracked. Romeo kept the intensity up on the sidelines and was hoping against all odds that his boys could keep their stamina up.

Bundy did score late in the first half despite the rantings of the Lizard Woman on the sidelines. A couple of police officers had ventured to the edge of the Heat Wave sideline, but each time they tried to come closer, Hector flared up and hissed at them.

The first half ended with Heat Wave leading 14–7. The Bundy Wolves tromped off to the shelter of their fancy locker room under the new stadium. Romeo Fleming, the Heat Wave Lizards, Hector, Aurora, and Lizard Woman sat in the rain in a circle under the wooden bleachers. Romeo stood in the middle of the players with a clipboard. The ten plays the Lizards knew had all faded down from the wet legal pad.

"If you believe it will, it will come true. It doesn't matter what's on this paper," he said. Then he tore off the pages and crumpled them in his hand. "As long as it's in your head and your heart."

Alice sat among them in her Lizard Woman outfit feeling the power of the circle. Meanwhile the Bundy band played an off-key rendition of "We'll Sing in the Sunshine" as they marched through the mud.

"Coach, those rednecks are really giving Willett a

hard time. You wouldn't believe the crap they're yelling at him. It's embarrassing,'' Bill Purdy said.

''Does it make you mad?'' Romeo asked.

''Hell, yes, it does,'' Billy fairly screamed.

''Good.''

''Sticks and stones may break my bones, but names jus' make me wanna score more touchdowns,'' Willett said.

Romeo smiled. ''Now just look up at the scoreboard one time,'' he said. ''We're beating the number one team in the state, but you'll have to pace yourselves, because they're probably going to come out fuming. We've made them look pretty bad in front of the home crowd. Let's make them look worse.''

Alice jumped up and grabbed Hector's leash and led the team back onto the field. Aurora ran beside her. She had nearly lost her voice. ''You make a wonderful-looking Lizard Woman, sister of mine, but watch out for Hector. I think he's falling in love.''

''Cute, real cute,'' Alice hissed from inside the big head.

Romeo Fleming was right. Bundy came out fired up. The head coach had given Glenn Tidwell a talking to on the sidelines right before the start of the second half. These lowlifes from the swamp had hit him hard and were playing smart defense, which meant he had tried to think, and thinking was a big problem for Glenn. They had made him look bad in front of the home fans, his wife, two children, and especially Billy Jean, the head cheerleader, who at that very moment was oogling at him and wetting her lips with her tongue.

Glenn fought his hardest not to think and led his team out of the huddle to begin the second half. The rain had turned to a hazy mist, but he managed to move Bundy for the first time against the Heat Wave defense. Then he got a tremendous assist from a very bad pass interference call by the referee. Alice went crazy when the referee dropped the flag, and she was now stalking behind him on the sidelines in her red lizard getup. "You'll burn in hell for that call!" she screamed. "I curse you to be torn apart by mongrel dogs."

Unfortunately, while Alice was tongue-lashing the referee, Heat Wave fumbled deep in its own territory. Glenn Tidwell faked everybody out on a perfect bootleg and ran twenty yards for the score yelling "Don't think, don't think!" as he crossed the goal line. Bundy finally took the lead 21–14. The crowd roared its approval.

The field now looked like a giant bowl of chocolate pudding. Neither team was able to move the ball—traction was nearly impossible. Aurora was now on the sideline next to Romeo holding the clipboard.

"Tell them to take their shoes off and play like they're in the sand," she told Romeo. So Romeo called time and had the team do it to the howl of the crowd. Heat Wave was faced with a fourth and five at the fifteen.

"Feels like it's secret weapon time to me," Romeo said.

Aurora told the rest of the bench to gather around them. Romeo then sent four players into the game, but five players came out. Balls Rawls stood on the sidelines just in bounds in front of Romeo. Heat Wave broke the huddle, and Billy Purdy went back to pass. Balls took off down the sidelines undetected by the Bundy secondary. Billy Purdy lofted a soggy spiral pass right to him in the end zone. Aurora's secret weapon had worked. Heat Wave made the extra point, and the game was tied.

The players celebrated on the sidelines, but Romeo was intense. He yelled to Alice, "See if you can conjure up another minute and a half of something to help us hang on."

Alice looked across the field at the packed grandstand and could feel the increasing hostility of the crowd. The thugs who heckled the team before had now reassembled near the end zone.

"You know if we win, they're going to try to kill us," she said to Romeo.

"That thought has crossed my mind."

"Not to worry, Coach," the Lizard Woman mused.

Bundy got the ball back with under two minutes to play, and Glenn Tidwell was still doing a pretty good job not thinking. The Heat Wave defense was wearing down. Bundy had been substituting fresh linemen against the only line Heat Wave had. Glenn mixed his plays well. To make matters worse, the rain had stopped, the ground fog had dissipated, and this opened up Glenn's deadly passing game.

Bundy was on the Heat Wave eleven-yard line with a first down and three time-outs when Romeo Fleming called his last time-out to rest his players. Boring Alice took advantage to gather the things she needed from the storage room. She was working frantically under the stands when the referee blew the whistle.

Romeo and Aurora were pacing the sidelines nervously as Bundy broke the huddle. The Heat Wave defense buckled up for the final attack. Glenn Tidwell handed off to his big fullback on a cross back, but the

Land Sharks were smelling blood and nailed the runner for no gain.

On second down Tidwell faked into the line and threw a screen pass to his halfback, who ran out of bounds at the nine. Glenn Tidwell ground his teeth and looked up at the scoreboard. There were just four seconds left.

"Don't think, don't think," he repeated to himself. Then he saw the kicking team about to come onto the field. "Screw that," he said aloud.

Oblivious to the hysterical group of coaches on the sideline, Glenn hurried the offense out of the huddle. "Fuck that goddamn kangaroo kicker," he thought to himself. This was *his* moment of glory, and he would take the team in for the winning touchdown.

On the Heat Wave sideline, Boring Alice was getting herself in position. Glenn Tidwell took the snap and dropped back looking for a receiver. Balls Rawls had slipped in the mud, and his man was wide open in the end zone. The lanky quarterback smiled and cocked his arm to throw the touchdown pass.

But he was momentarily distracted by the crazy woman in the lizard suit. She was waving a sign with his name on it, and he tried to *think*—to comprehend what it said. That was the split second Dr. Boom needed to reach him. At full speed, Dr. Boom came running from his middle linebacker position and leveled Glenn Tidwell, knocking him into next week.

The ball flew out of Glenn's outstretched hand and stayed in the air for what seemed like an eternity. And then it was plucked out of the sky by Willett Rainer Snow, who raced down the sidelines and scored the winning touchdown.

* * *

After the game, as they celebrated in the end zone, a mob, including the coaches, cops, and referees, came from the other end of the field and surrounded them. Hector could feel the threatening vibes and went into his attack posture. That scattered a good portion of the throng so Alice could drive the bus onto the field and pick them all up. She ran every red light and did not slow down until the smell of the paper mill was out of her nostrils.

She drove the bus up to the Northern Lights, and they all went in and continued the victory party. Romeo had bought a case of beer on the causeway for his warriors, and they drank and sprayed it on each other as if they had won the World Series. They hung the red lizard skin from the ceiling and thanked the lizard gods for delivering them safely home.

The jukebox was blasting, and Alice danced with the entire team as Jerry Lee Lewis sang "Whole Lotta Shakin' Goin' On." Aurora cooked cheeseburgers, and Romeo sat at the counter enjoying the moment. Hector was stretched out in front of the door. "I remember one of those fools yelling, 'Godzilla is attacking! Call the National Guard!' " He laughed again, spewing a mouthful of beer.

"If the rest of your schedule is anything like this, I'm demanding combat pay for going to the games," Aurora told him.

"Combat pay, hell," Romeo replied, "you'll be fined if you don't show up. Those are the rules for an assistant coach. I'm afraid we've created a monster, and I could use a little help."

Aurora was overwhelmed with the offer. Tears welled up as she flipped a burger and looked at her sister and the team jitterbugging on the tables. "I see a whole room full of monsters, and you're right. You *are* gonna need some help."

The party wrapped up around one o'clock, and Romeo drove the bus over to the school and dropped off his players. Aurora and Boring Alice walked home together as the waning moon rose in the early morning sky over the empty streets of Heat Wave. They walked in silence through town, and when they turned on the Gulf Road for home, Alice Porter looked at her sister and asked, "By the way, what was on that poster you held up?"

Boring Alice started to giggle. "It said 'GLENN TIDWELL CAN NOT READ THIS SIGN.' " Aurora stopped in her tracks and burst out laughing.

Boring Alice kept on walking down the sandy street and began to sing that old song from long ago, "Déjà, déjà, déjà vu." And from behind her Aurora answered, "Believe it, and it will come true."

BOOMERANG LOVE

Angel Beech was home. She could smell the pungent aroma of the exposed mud flats of Perdido Bay as she handed her driver's license to the deputy sheriff directing southbound traffic on the causeway leading to Snake Bite Key.

In the opposite lane, a long line of cars, trailers, and trucks slowly moved north, away from the low-lying barrier islands. A serious hurricane warning had been issued earlier in the day; now the weatherman on the radio gave the latitude and longitude of Hurricane Saba, who was plodding northward through the Gulf of Mexico on her way to an inevitable landfall somewhere on the Gulf Coast. She had been spawned off of the Azores and had raced west over the Atlantic Ocean, gaining strength as she sideswiped the Virgin Islands and slammed directly into Jamaica and across Oriente Province in Cuba out into the open waters of the Gulf.

At the present time, the storm was one hundred and

seventy-five miles south of Pascagoula, speeding in a northeasterly direction at fifteen miles per hour. Winds were about one hundred and thirty knots, and tides were ten feet above normal. Angel's hometown, Heat Wave, Alabama, was about to get the living shit kicked out of it.

Angel thought about what the weatherman had said. Eighty percent of the people who now lived on the Gulf Coast had never seen a hurricane. These were the people in the cars she passed, getting the hell out of Dodge to find safety in the Holiday Inns of Birmingham. Yet for some strange reason, she was driving straight into the eye of the storm.

"You're a long way from California, ma'am. The road is closed except to residents of the islands," the young man drawled.

"I'm from Heat Wave," Angel told him.

The young man laughed and shook his head. "You sure picked a hell of a time to come visiting."

Angel took her license back from the deputy and smiled. "I'm not visiting. I've come to protect what's mine. My father used to be the mayor of Heat Wave—Conrad Beech."

The young man immediately recognized the name and motioned her through with a word of caution. "This storm's supposed to be worse than that storm way back in the fifties, and we can't be responsible for your safety if you stay."

"Thank you, Officer, but I've been working without a net for quite some time." Angel rolled up her window and hit the gas, leaving the bewildered deputy behind.

She drove across the causeway and saw the new golf course that had been built on the north side of Little

Billy Creek. She turned right and circled the island, passing the monument erected after the last killer storm, the one that had taken her mother. She drove past Bar-B-Q Hill and saw the old Patterson house boarded up tight. After parking the Jeep, she climbed to the top of the hill and looked out at the water.

Beyond the dunes, the sea was dark, and whitecaps streaked along the surface like whipped cream. The smell of pine straw, the tide, and the sea brought Angel's childhood memories up from the well of her being, and she thought about her mother, her father, Catholic school, fishing trips, and a hundred memories of growing up. She carefully stepped through rocks and sand back down to the car and headed for town, stopping at the familiar old weather-beaten sign that marked the entrance to town. The sign swayed in the wind. "Welcome to Heat Wave. Bake until done, then go home."

Her father had painted it in his workshed, just after he'd successfully convinced the locals not to rename the town. This was back when the first bankers and land developers from Mobile were trying to cash in on the island. Her father had taken them on and beaten them. Still, it saddened her to know they had finally gotten a foothold when they built the Soft Shell Golf and Country Club. As her father used to say, "If you were goin' on vacation or tryin' to find a place to retire to and was lookin' at the Texaco road map to find a spot, what sounds better: Heat Wave on Snake Bite Key or Silver Springs?"

The argument had worked while he was alive, but it seemed nobody could just leave well enough alone. Yet the town of Heat Wave had fought the onslaught of condo commandos just over the bridge; they were spreading like a plague across the rest of the Gulf Coast. For generations Angel's family had prevailed on Snake Bite Key. It was *her* turf, and she knew it well. Now nature was in motion, and the fury of a big storm was not going to discriminate between environmentalist or developer when it came ashore.

Angel Beech had been named for one of her father's favorite fishing spots. Conrad Beech, former Navy pilot, local fishing guide, and mayor of Heat Wave, was given the task of raising his only daughter from the age of three, when her mother had been swept away from them by the killer hurricane of 1953. That storm, named Blanche, had scooped up a ten-mile-long, two-mile-wide stretch of sand, home, and humans and hurled them all into the sea. Conrad had lived through it, swimming the entire night with his daughter on his back searching in vain for his precious wife until huge tides had fallen and Heat Wave had been separated from the peninsula. The survivors of the storm erected a monument to their lost loved ones, but nobody moved away. The locals picked up the pieces and started over again.

"I'm glad I never had a son," Conrad used to tell his daughter. "First of all, he'd have to go through a lot of crap at school bein' called 'son of a beech,' and besides, I'm not sure the world or me would be quite ready for another me. Sons and wives can scatter like the wind and never be seen or heard from again, but your daughter is always your daughter."

Angel wiped tears away and laughed aloud, remembering her father. She leaned her slender body into a wind so forceful it kept her from falling. Somewhere out in this mixture of brown water and gray swirling clouds, the souls of the people who had brought her into the world seemed to be calling her home. What was the reason? Why had she left Los Angeles in the middle of an important business dinner at Spago and immediately booked a flight to New Orleans when she heard of the storm?

Maybe it was the way the TV weatherman had joked about such names as Snake Bite Key and Heat Wave. She knew, despite his tone, that they weren't cute, made-up places. They were real; they were her past. And in the world of L.A. deals and dollars, very few things were real.

If there was one real thing she had, it was a wonderful, almost magical past: a beautiful, unknown mother who she dreamed of as a mermaid, a father who hung the moon, and a true gypsy love lost to a meandering soul he couldn't control. Now the only real men in her life were just memories. One, her father, was dead, and the other, Hannah, was no doubt somewhere over China. Many times she had wondered about Hannah Hearndon's whereabouts, for her years in New Orleans and California had produced a few pleasurable, torrid affairs with little substance.

She drove down the main street of Heat Wave for the first time in five years, and a lump welled up in her throat as she remembered the last time she saw her father: they had gone night fishing for sharks on Angel Beach. She had come home from New Orleans immediately, when Conrad's first mate, Lincoln Shivers, called about her father's heart attack. Her father claimed it was nothing but a bad oyster, and had himself out of the hospital in a day.

Conrad wanted to take her out fishing that night. It was the new moon, and the incoming tide would spawn a lot of life in the food chain. They drove his old pickup out onto Angel Beach and stopped at the monument to toss a red rose into the sea, a tribute to her mother. They fished all night and drank beer, and Conrad talked of his flying days out in the Pacific and how he and her mother met at the officers' club in Honolulu. He was still in love with her. Then he retold the story of the storm.

They had brought Conrad's small telescope, and Angel stared at the rings around Saturn, mesmerized by the vision.

"See, Daddy, if you think California is far away, what the hell would you do if I moved to Saturn?" she asked.

"I have a feeling I'd feel a lot more comfortable about you living on Saturn than out in Hollyweird. How a girl raised to be the first female captain on the coast wound up as a French Quarter beatnik and then ran off to California to paint sets for movin' pictures is still beyond me," Conrad said.

"It's what I want to do, Daddy," Angel told him.

"Just like your mother." Conrad smiled.

They hooked up a big fish as the sky was showing the slightest bit of morning color to the east, and Conrad asked Angel to run up to the bait shop and get him some fresh coffee and a pack of cheese crackers. She was concerned. She could see his whole body tense up as he played the big fish on the handline, but he insisted he was fine.

When Angel returned, she saw her father and the giant hammerhead shark rolling in the shallow surf like dead soldiers on a beachhead.

Two days later, she was scattering his ashes over the monument and saying a prayer. Her mother and father were finally together again and could be happy for the rest of eternity.

The next day Lincoln Shivers drove her to Mobile to catch a plane to California. She wondered all the way out West if Conrad had sent her for coffee so she wouldn't see him die.

Angel pulled the Jeep into the oyster-shell driveway of her father's house. The wind was blowing the magnolia and pine trees around in a bizarre dance. Her father and Lincoln Shivers had built this house after Hurricane Blanche. It was specially designed to withstand any storm, and it sat ten feet above the ground on steel poles embedded in concrete caulker dams. The roof was held down by cables that could be tightened to keep it from blowing off. This was home.

She saw Lincoln Shivers down on the wharf working on the *Miss Steph*, her father's old charter boat. Lincoln inherited it from Conrad and was now the captain.

He saw her, waved, and started to run to the house.

"Stay there, Lincoln!" she shouted and jumped back into the Jeep. She drove to the water, hopped out of her car, and ran down the wharf to the boat and leaped on deck into the outstretched arms of the giant black man.

"My, Miss Angel, you are as pretty as you ever was," he whispered.

Angel looked at Lincoln. He never seemed to age. And it was just like him to have kept the old boat so beautifully maintained.

"She looks as good as ever, and the house, too. God bless you and thank you, Lincoln, for watching out for them. Do you know there are people in California who would pay a fortune for your secret to staying so young?"

"Oh, Angel! Ocean air with a little dash of wine, women, and song—that ain't no secret at all," he said, laughing. "But now I got to be gettin' this boat up the creek here sometime soon to the hurricane hole, but I was waitin' for you to get here before I went. Somehow I knew you'd be back."

Together they walked up to the house.

"You know, Lincoln, I forget sometimes how wonderful it is here. I needed this storm. I couldn't bring myself to come back here 'cause it seemed so empty without Daddy around, but I've missed you."

She inhaled slowly and held the humid air and aromas of cedar and pine and low tide inside her for a long time. Then she let them go.

"I can smell this place in my dreams."

"Well, we're gonna be smellin' hell and high water if this here hurricane gets hold of us, 'cause they say it be worse than that one that drowned your poor mama."

"Well, let's batten down the hatches then, mate," Angel said. "We don't have much time."

Together they covered the screen porch and all the windows with numbered storm boards. It took them a while to rig up the maze of extension cords to the emergency generator, but after that the house was secured. The little boat was still in the water, but Angel told Lincoln she could take care of it.

"What a saint you are, to have done all this," she said.

She waved from the wharf as Lincoln took the *Miss Steph* up Little Billy Creek past Delaney's boatyard to his house. There he would weave a protective web of lines and anchors around the old boat to ride out the storm. He had volunteered to come back and stay with Angel in the house, but she told him she would be fine, and she wanted him to stay with his boat—she knew he would have done that if she hadn't been there.

She went inside the boathouse and found her namesake tied off to a deck cleat like a gentle horse at a hitching post. The *Angel Baby* was hers. Her father built the little cypress skiff himself and gave it to her on her tenth birthday. That day, the *Angel Baby* had been tied in exactly the same spot with a big red ribbon running the length of the deck and a giant card taped to the seat, which read: "Your first yacht. Love, Dad."

She touched the weathered wheel. She had spent most of her growing-up days in that boat.

Angel glanced at her watch when the clock in the boathouse rang eight bells, and she knew she had better get to town before the stores closed. She let off a little slack on the lines as the tide began to rise, and she hurried back to the Jeep. She waved to everyone she saw as she passed the waterfront, and though they all were in a hurry, they all waved back. She felt as if she had never left the coast.

Angel went to Lumpkin's for groceries, remembering her father's words as she shopped. "If I'm about to eat my last meal and meet my Maker, then I'm sure as hell not goin' out on a bellyful of goddamn Spam."

She bought steaks and fresh oysters and vegetables and lots of ice and water and a bottle of rum. She loaded the groceries into the Jeep and walked next door to the marine supply store. There she filled her shopping cart with new mantles for the hurricane lamps, and batteries for the flashlights, stereo, and VHF radios. In the process of provisioning, she ran into Sister Mary Margaret, her second-grade teacher, and Hannah Hearndon.

Hannah Hearndon, the only man she had ever really been in love with, was holding a handful of spark plugs and talking to Kirk Patterson, a local fishing captain. Hannah left her life as abruptly as he entered it. One balmy summer afternoon in 1967, when she was seventeen, she lay naked in the sun in a secluded little cove on the west end of the island, and he floated down out of the sky. Hannah was in Navy flight school in Pensacola and had to eject from his trainer when the engine caught on fire.

"This sort of takes the mystery out of things."

These were the first words he had spoken to her, scanning her young body before she sprang up and ran for the bushes.

They were a couple from the start, and Conrad and Hannah got along the way fliers do. It was a glorious summer, and Hannah and Angel were together nearly every day.

There were a lot of "firsts" with this man. First motorcycle ride, first airplane ride, first love. She had lost her virginity to Hannah, which in those days was supposed to mean something. But the war changed all that. He was soon flying F-4s off an aircraft carrier in Vietnam, and she was off to college in New Orleans, painting on the sidewalk in front of the St. Louis Cathedral.

While Angel was in New Orleans, her father just showed up one day and found her sketching at her easel outside Jackson Square. She knew it wasn't a social visit. They went to Tujague's and ate gumbo and brisket, and after two bottles of wine, he told her Hannah had been shot down and was missing.

"Thanks for letting me eat first," Angel said. Then she cried in her father's arms until she fell asleep.

But Hannah Hearndon survived the crash and walked out of the highlands of Vietnam to the coast, where he strolled into a bar looking like Tarzan and ordered a beer as if nothing had happened. None of this was known to Angel, who had worked very hard at accepting Hannah's death. All of it added to the shock the day she heard the buzzer of her little apartment on Ursuline Street ring and opened the door to see Hannah standing there in his dress whites.

"Fats Domino is playing at the Blue Room, and I got two tickets if you'd like to go."

They missed the Fats Domino show and everything else in town. Instead, they locked themselves in Angel's apartment in the French Quarter and made love in the sweltering heat of a New Orleans summer, going out only to pick up Muffalata sandwiches and Dixie Beer from the Central Grocery on Decatur Street. Hannah finished out his hitch in the Navy as an instructor in Pensacola and drove his motorcycle to New Orleans every weekend.

Angel was in love for the first and last time in her life. There was no one else for her but Hannah, and she would have tossed away all her plans for the future to spend her life with him. He was fun, and smart, and sensitive, and a provocative lover—but he was a loner. So one day she came home to a short note that simply said this: though he loved her more than any woman he had ever met, he was happiest when he was on the move. He had bought a small sailboat and was on his way to Tahiti.

There were a few postcards from exotic places over the years, and a letter of condolence from Argentina was delivered to her in California a month after Conrad's death. Over the past few years, she had once again almost put him out of her mind—but here he was, only a few feet from her.

He stopped talking to Kirk.

"Hi," he said.

"Hi," she said back.

"You here for the storm?" he asked.

Angel just nodded.

Hannah smiled, and twenty years melted away. She felt as if she were back on the beach, just standing there physically and emotionally naked for all the world to see.

Hurricane Saba was winding up tighter in the Gulf, pulling all the bad weather for hundreds of miles together toward her eye. The sandy streets of the tiny fishing village were empty, and the buildings were boarded up tight. All awaited the onslaught of wind and sea.

Not a gull flew in the gray sky, no dog barked on land, and the barometric pressure dropped steadily as darkness advanced. It was the calm before the storm.

The sight of Hannah—in the marine supply store in the middle of Heat Wave in the path of a hurricane—got to Angel. She asked him to take her for a drink at the Homeport Bar.

The little bar on the beach was a time capsule. When

they entered, both were greeted by old friends who asked if Angel needed any help securing her house. No questions or smoldering glances or gossip in the corner. This was one of the nice things about Heat Wave. It was home, and your business was your business.

A hurricane party was in progress. The atmosphere was carnival-like, as patrons sang, drank, and joked about the upcoming storm that could possibly kill them all. To the locals, hurricanes were simply a part of life and death.

Angel and Hannah moved past the crowded bar to a table near the window facing southeast out over the Gulf. No one bothered them.

"He hasn't aged that much," Angel thought, "except for the crow's-feet." As always, his impish eyes hid his true thoughts and secrets from almost everyone. Hannah was a complicated individual but not hard for Angel to figure out.

He didn't speak to her while they ordered drinks. He kept his eyes on the sky and the horizon and scanned the island as if he had antennae telling him what he needed to know.

"You here for the storm, Angel?" he asked again.

"I could ask you the same question."

There was a moment of silence. "Play or pass," Angel said, and that broke the ice. They laughed together as if on cue.

Hannah lifted his drink for a toast, and Angel accepted it. "I'll play," he said. "First of all, I'm sorry about Conrad. I got the word when I was in South America and thought about coming back then and trying to find you, but something came up. I don't know why I came now. I have a little seaplane charter business down in Costa Rica, moving fishermen from the Río Colorado to Flamingo and back. I've been there for about three years now, the longest I've been in any one place since Vietnam.

"Well, some old fart from Missouri gave me a big tip after we jumped twelve tarpon one afternoon, and I decided to buy a satellite dish. The boys who worked for me were real excited about the Playboy channel, but I was more interested in the weather channel. After all, we were a long way from civilization. There was a lot of excitement around the house when the thing was delivered, and when we got it hooked together and fired it up, the first thing that came on was the hurricane report.

"I watched the tape loop of the storm passing over Cuba into the Gulf and heard them say it was on its way to the Panhandle. I hadn't thought much about Heat Wave in years, and then, all of a sudden, I had this strange feeling that I . . . ah." He paused, not able to finish his train of thought.

Angel finished it for him. "You didn't want the storm to hit without you being here."

"Exactly." Hannah sighed. "And you?"

"I needed some excitement in my life. Once again, I'd worked you out of my system and had accomplished what I set out to do career-wise, but something was missing. Did you ever think you would see me again?"

He put his drink down. "I was flying up over Mexico, and when I crossed the border into Texas, I saw this colossal shooting star tumble out of the dark with a tail that lit up half the sky. I made my wish, and here you are."

Angel touched his face. "I could use some help with the skiff," she said.

When they got back to the house, they loaded the *Angel Baby* onto the trailer and hauled her up the hill to the workshed and tucked her away. Angel and Hannah stared at the boat for a while. Then Angel broke the silence.

"Hannah, I know what you're thinking about, 'cause I'm thinking about it, too. Come on, let's go. I've got a last supper to make."

Lincoln had kept the old house in as good shape as Conrad had, and the kitchen came alive. Angel lit the burners, and soon the old, familiar smell of simmering garlic and onions permeated every room. The electricity was still on, and Hannah placed a Glenn Miller album on the turntable of the old Magnavox. They did not talk much. Over the many years of this boomerang love, they had learned to communicate without speaking.

Hannah found a chart of the Gulf and was plotting the coordinates of the storm while the man on the portable radio read them out. Angel lifted biscuits out of the oven and stirred the oysters into steaming hot milk. She added some fresh chives and a few shakes of Tabasco sauce to cook up a simple, delicious oyster stew.

"It looks like landfall for Miss Saba will be around midnight, somewhere on Snake Bite Key, probably Heat Wave."

Angel put the broiled steaks on china plates. With Hannah keeping a watchful eye on the storm, she felt safe as ever in this old house. "Let's eat," she called. "Oh shit, we forgot to get wine." But then she perked up. "Wait a minute, wait a minute." The words trailed behind her as she disappeared into Conrad's room. "Hannah," she called. "Bring me a flashlight, please."

Hannah brought a light and found her rummaging in her father's closet and heard her yell, "Thank you, Daddy dear." She had found the old man's wine stash—about twenty bottles of 1959 Grand Echézeaux. She kissed Hannah quickly on the lips as she passed by and said, "Dinner is served."

The last supper was exquisite, and the wine set the mood for the night. It had started to rain, and the wind was blowing a gale outside, adding an eerie chorus to the refrains of "Moonlight Serenade" coming from the stereo.

They sat together at the kitchen counter, and Angel lay her last piece of steak on Hannah's plate. He accepted it with a smile, but he didn't eat it. She emptied her glass of Burgundy and felt it travel down her throat without the slightest bite.

The wine let the words flow up from her heart. "Hannah Hearndon," she said, "if you put on brakes tonight, honey, you'd skid for twenty years."

The lights in the house flickered, then went out for good. Glenn Miller took a break. The glow of the hurricane lamp in the kitchen made them visible to each other.

"This is no chance meeting," Hannah said. "This was meant to happen. I think about you all the time, but I don't know what to do about you."

"You don't have to do anything. I don't want to own you. I never could. We must be meant to stay in motion—but you in your orbit and me in mine. And, if occasionally our paths cross, we'll make the most of it.'' Angel found Hannah's hand in the dim light and stood up. ''Let's check out this storm,'' she whispered softly in his ear. Hannah stopped at Conrad's desk, and Angel let go of his hand. She opened the door to the sound of the hurricane and stepped outside.

The wind gauge above the old desk read forty knots. The barometer had dropped half an inch since Hannah last checked it. He turned the face of the barometer to the wall. ''No need for that anymore,'' he thought. He went outside to find Angel.

A full moon was shining intermittently through rapidly moving low clouds, and it looked like the sweep of a lighthouse beacon. He heard the sound of running water and slowly walked to the end of the porch, looking down to find out what was making the noise.

The outdoor shower was on. He could hear Angel humming a song, and then the moon appeared momentarily, illuminating the night. Light shimmered across Angel's long body, and Hannah could see it had not lost its shape one bit. Her breasts stood straight out, and he watched as she moved the bar of soap in circles around her nipples.

Angel closed her eyes to let the soap flow out of her hair. She had forgotten the luxury of bathing outside in the open air. She turned down the cold water and let hot steamy water pound against the back of her neck. She never saw Hannah enter the shower; she only felt him come up behind her and press himself next to her, biting her gently on the earlobe.

Suddenly a gust of wind blew and threw them down. They didn't get up for a long time. They made love over and over, as lightning flashed and the tide rose over the wharf.

The mounting storm fueled their passion with a fearless energy neither could believe. They felt a part of the tumultuous night. The storm tide moved the sea halfway up the big yard, and a three-foot swell broke over the bulkhead. They went body surfing, riding the misplaced surf as far into the yard as they could and then rolled and splashed in the water like mating dolphins. Angel sensed the worlds of land and sea colliding, with them in the middle.

Hannah took Angel in his arms and walked through the waist-high water down to the boathouse and gently lowered her onto the wicker couch. He found a sail bag in the loft and wrapped it around her. He held her tight and closed his eyes and saw himself as a boomerang, soaring out over the songlines of the universe for what seemed like an eternity. Lying next to Angel, he felt himself making the big turn back to where he came from.

The spirits of the victims of the great storm of 1953, led by Angel Beech's mother, must have been working their magic to full intensity that night, because around midnight, Hurricane Saba made an unexpected turn to the east, sparing Heat Wave from the full force of the storm. Instead, the big storm went ashore just east of Destin and hugged the shoreline, scouring the coastline clean before she moved across northern Florida and back out into the Atlantic.

Politicians flew around in helicopters and declared the coast a disaster area, but a lot of old-timers were happy the storm had come. Gone were the high rises and miniature golf courses and video arcades. The shoreline was once again the way it had been.

Hannah Hearndon opened his eyes to a sparkling

dawn. A small line of rain squalls hovered over the harbor, and a double rainbow arced down out of the clouds to the shore. He woke Angel to show her the incredible scene. They were not dead; they had lived through another storm, and the memories of their night were somewhere between fact and fantasy. The water had receded to its original shore, and the blue sky was filled with seabirds. Heat Wave had survived.

They went inside and dressed. Angel gave some of her father's old clothes to Hannah. She made them café au lait, and they sat again at the kitchen counter amid the supper dishes.

Hannah ate the last piece of cold steak off his dinner plate. "The deal was you cook and I clean up, but I got a little sidetracked last night." He began to wash the dishes, and Angel just sat at the counter watching him, sipping her coffee.

"You don't look right doing that," she said. "Too domestic."

"Well, I try not to make a habit of it," Hannah told her. "And a lot of other things."

"I just want you to know what happened last night doesn't change how I feel about you. I won't be the same for days, mind you, but it doesn't mean I have to live with you." She got up and walked behind the counter and put her arms around him.

He leaned down and kissed her softly, holding his dishpan hands up in the air. "I'm tired of moving," he said, "and this place looks like it could use a little work. I want to . . ."

The Glenn Miller orchestra unhastily started up on the record player and interrupted him, for the power had suddenly come back on. Angel burst out laughing. "So much for that idea! I guess somebody up there is trying to tell you something, honey." The embarrassed, puzzled look on Hannah's face was not one Angel had seen before, but she let it go without comment. After Hannah finished up the dishes, he and Angel went outside to survey the damage. With the exception of a few downed pine trees, the place had come through in good shape. They heard news of the change in the storm's course on the radio while they were raking the yard and cutting away fallen trees.

Lincoln returned midmorning on the *Miss Steph*, surprised as hell, but glad to see Hannah. A county sheriff's car pulled into the driveway, and the deputy Angel had talked to the day before got out of the car just to check their situation.

The *Angel Baby*, lowered back into the water, started up on the first try. They passed the Homeport Bar and saw survivors of the party coming out and heading home. The Gulf was like a mirror, and the full moon was still shining at midday.

Angel and Hannah were going to stay in Heat Wave for a while. Then Angel thought she might go back to L.A. to finish the movie she was working on, but she wasn't sure. The storm had brought her life into a little better focus. She didn't feel desperate to find a man anymore, and the fantasy of Hollywood couldn't hold a candle to the real-life world where she was born.

She thought of her father. "Women," he would say, "are the guardians of continuity. If the hearth moves, they move with it. Remember, it is the gypsy women who keep their men on the road."

Hannah helped her pull the boat onto the shore near the old monument. It, too, had survived another storm. They walked out to the point, and Angel tossed a rose into the tranquil waters of the Gulf. "Thanks, Mom and Dad," she called out.

Hannah took her hand and they walked back to the boat. "The Neville Brothers are playing in New Orleans tonight, and I got a couple of tickets," he said.

"The man just can't stand still!" she yelled at the sky. Angel reached into the bow of the boat, picked up the small anchor, and handed it to Hannah. "It's not that heavy," she said.

He began to pull slowly on the line and let it fall into the surf. "Seems to be a lot of slack, too," he replied.

"Well, if the line's too tight, it could snap at any time, and I would lose a good ship."

Hannah pushed the *Angel Baby* off the beach. He handed her the anchor. "No, it doesn't seem too heavy at all," he said.

Angel lifted the sail quickly, and they caught an offshore breeze and disappeared past the point—where the red rose turned slowly around and around in the changing tide.

THE SWAMP CREATURE LET ONE IN

It was not a month for eatin' oysters. Any way you spelled it, it was hotter than the hinges of hell. Snake Bite Key baked in a steamy coastal haze like a hush-puppy in a microwave. Crickets in the cypress trees put out a racket that nearly equaled the decibel level of the hundreds of air conditioners in nearby condos.

You would have been hard pressed to convince early French explorers who ''discovered'' this isthmus that it was prime Sun Belt real estate. But alas, anything was possible toward the end of the twentieth century.

Still, this was the cool, cool, cool of evening on Snake Bite Key—the only time for real sportsmen to be on the fairways of the new back nine at the Soft Shell Golf and Country Club.

Two custom golf carts were parked next to the sixteenth tee. A man wearing an orange-and-pink Hawaiian shirt and Vietnamese jungle shorts poured himself a big drink from the portable bar attached to his camouflaged golf cart. The sportsman's name was Eugene "Balls" Rawls, former free safety for the Heat Wave High Lizards and the only millionaire in town. He was *not* in a good mood. Once again, Balls was losing to his nemesis, "Lard Ass" Louis Huckle, a carpetbagger charcoal baron, a recent transplant from the North.

Balls's family had lived on Snake Bite Key since the migration from Arcadia in the eighteenth century. Thanks to his grandfather, who had invented a shrimp-peeling apparatus, he had managed to avoid real work for most of his life. Balls had spent most of his time fishing, but when the country club was built, he joined and took up golf. He could never quite figure out why he had switched from the tranquility of fishing to the mindless frustration of golf, especially when he was playing with someone like Lard Ass. It must have been because he wanted to teach the obnoxious old fart a little lesson in humility.

At the moment this wasn't working, for now Balls faced the hole he feared most—hole number sixteen, which had reduced his life expectancy more than booze or cigarettes. In his five years playing the course, Balls had *never* landed on the green of number sixteen. He always went into the lake on the right.

Willett Rainer Snow, the head caddie and fairway supervisor, enjoyed watching Balls and Lard Ass play golf as much as he liked watching "All My Children," though in his estimation the soap opera had lost a lot of punch since the demise of Billy Clyde Tuggle and Ray Gardner. Willett had known Balls since they were kids. He, too, was hoping that one day a miracle would happen and Balls would humble Lard Ass.

Willett and Balls had played football together in a

glorious season nearly a quarter of a century earlier when a part-time English teacher named Romeo Fleming coached the Lizards to an undefeated season and the Alabama State Championship. Willett had been one of the first black players for Bear Bryant at the University of Alabama, but his career was cut short by a knee injury. He returned home and had gone back to shrimping until the golf course came along.

He took up caddying not because he knew anything about golf but because the course was closer to home. He had only played golf once, and that was at a putt putt course. His change of career came about like this: when the Soft Shell Golf and Country Club had been carved out of the coastal swamp, the architects, designers, and builders forgot to tell the large indigenous population of water moccasins that their home was now high-priced real estate, and they would have to leave.

Willett seized the opportunity and offered for an exorbitant price—to get rid of the snakes. At first Forrest Clockwork, the manager, declined. Then a prospective buyer was bitten while looking for his fluorescent golf ball in the rough. Suddenly the price seemed very reasonable. Willett hauled so many cottonmouths out he had to use dump trucks, and he was paid quite well. And then, seeing what a valuable commodity Willett was to his "investment," Forrest Clockwork made Willett Rainer Snow the head caddie and fairway supervisor. This met with some hostile reactions from the membership committee since Willett knew nothing about golf and wouldn't carry a golf bag. But Forrest reminded them how much money was involved in the project and how easily it could all go down the drain if one more prospective customer became a pincushion for a water moccasin family. If the members of the committee had any further complaints, they kept them to themselves.

Then came the ticks. It seems the snakes were not the only species of God's creatures to be upset by the human alteration of their habitat. Theirs was a species called the babyback tick by the locals. They attached themselves to swamp animals, dogs, and the few humans who ventured into the swamps, and they got their nourishment, usually without causing any harm. But when the country club and golf course were built and rich people began chasing their golf balls around, the babyback tick bite sent the six-figure victims into fevers and nausea that lasted for days.

Forrest again came to Willett for advice.

"Well, it seems to me that these here ticks only make rich people sick, so I'd suggest they try bein' poor, and if that don't work, tell 'em to hit the ball straight, and they won't have no problems. And if that don't work, call in the spray planes."

Soon the local crop dusters were flying low-level sorties over the golf course, and Willett had again been proved indispensable for his store of common sense—something that seemed to be lacking among the rich and powerful.

Willett soon started liking the game of golf, as badly as it was played at the Soft Shell Golf and Country Club. Sometimes in the late evenings, he and Balls played together and joked about the fact that most club members believed riding around in electric carts chasing a little white ball was good, healthy exercise. Willett spoke rarely and carried a big stick to clobber "Mr. No Shoulders," his name for a water moccasin.

Willett anointed himself with military mosquito repellent and watched Lard Ass step up to the sixteenth tee. Willett could truly understand Balls's quest to humble this genetic asshole, but unfortunately Lard Ass played consistent golf and was incredibly lucky. Balls never got a break, and he played left-handed.

Lard Ass waddled up and knelt to tee up the ball—bending over would have toppled his out-of-balance upper torso, and he might never get up again. Still, when Lard Ass hit the ball, it went straight, and today was no exception. His shot bounced in front of the green on number sixteen and rolled up twenty feet from the pin.

Balls finished his drink and teed up. He peered down the fairway toward Lard Ass's ball on the green.

"You sure you got enough aimin' fluid in ya?" Lard Ass asked. "You're shakin' like a hound dog shittin' peach seeds."

Balls was not amused. He stood over the ball and looked at Willett.

"What do the golf gods say about this sonofabitchin' hole today, Willett?"

Willett took the toothpick out of his mouth. "There ain't no golf god rules on this hole, Balls. This here's the Swamp Creature's territory."

"Hey, cut the bullshit and hit. We got heavy money ridin' on this hole," Lard Ass bellowed. Balls swung his seven iron back in a multicolored blur. He almost catapulted himself onto the green. The ball sailed about an inch above the manicured zoysia grass and skipped three times before it disappeared into the lake.

"Worm burner!" yelled Lard Ass. "Maybe you oughta try hittin' from the right side. I'll see you on the green.'' Lard Ass put the pedal to the metal of his shiny new canary-yellow imitation Rolls-Royce golf cart. The engine strained under his weight, and he giggled like a hyena as he zoomed to the green.

Balls walked slowly to his cart and rammed the seven iron back into the bag. ''I hate this goddamn game,'' he snarled. ''Why do I subject myself to that asshole?''

''Aw, he can't help it, Balls. He was just born that way. You'll get the best of him one day.'' Willett strolled off the tee and down the right side of the fairway, poking through the bushes with his big stick. He came to a stop and with lightning quickness whirled the stick over his head and down to the ground with a thud. Life ended for another Mr. No Shoulders.

The blender stopped, and the lights went out in the men's grill at the Soft Shell Golf and Country Club. A thunderclap shook the pine-paneled room. Lard Ass and Balls were now seated at the poker table in front of the big picture window.

''I believe that was one bet and two presses. Sorry I can't stay and have a drink, Balls, but if you don't mind, I'll just collect and get on home before 'Wheel of Fortune' starts.''

''The power is out, Lard Ass. No Vanna tonight,'' Balls said.

''Not so. I have a new, battery-operated Watchman. Got it at K Mart for ninety-nine dollars, a blue-light special. Jesus, it's dark in here.''

Just then Willett came into the room carrying a hissing hurricane lantern that cast contorted shadows on the walls of the whole room. ''What's going on?'' the bartender asked.

"Transformer got fried, but the generator should be kickin' in here quick." At that instant, the blender purred, and the lights came back on. "This be one bitchin' storm," Willett continued. "They got flash floods up in Fairhope, and a little twister done touched down at Orange Beach."

Balls pulled two hundred-dollar bills out of his wallet and gingerly tossed them across the mahogany poker table to Lard Ass, who snatched them up.

"Your game sucks, Balls, but in one respect we *do* play on an equal level. No one has ever made a hole in one on sixteen. Not even *me*."

"Five grand says I can take you on that hole," Balls said. A huge thunderclap rumbled in the distance.

"Did I hear you right, Balls?" Lard Ass began to laugh under his breath.

"You heard me right, Lard Ass. Be there tomorrow morning at eight, number sixteen. One hole, winner take all," Balls said coldly.

Lard Ass wasn't sure how to react, but he kept giggling. "It's your money, sonny. I'll be there." He waddled out of the room.

"Give my best to Vanna, and be sure to lock the bathroom door," Balls yelled.

Willett whistled softly and said, "I do believe that's the first time I've ever seen ol' Mr. Huckle at a loss for words."

Balls went over to the bar and gave the bartender a twenty. "I'll lock up," he said. The bartender was happy to leave and handed him the key.

Balls went behind the bar and reached up to the top shelf and pulled down a bottle of Glenlivet scotch. He picked up two glasses and went back to the poker table.

"Willett," he said as he poured, "I just bet that loud-mouthed sonofabitch five thousand dollars that I can beat him on a hole where I've never even made the green. I want to know why it looks so easy and is so goddamn hard. Do you think there's anything to that Swamp Creature shit?"

"It ain't shit, Balls. Do you know the real story?"

"Just the stuff I heard growin' up, but me an' the Swamp Creature have never met on a social basis."

"Do you believe in Santa Claus?" Willett asked.

"Sort of."

Willett rocked back in the rattan chair and put his feet up on the poker table. He bottomed up his glass of high-dollar scotch and took in a deep breath.

"Well, I think it's about time you heard the story. It started a long time before this highfalutin' crab trap of a country club was built, and just think about this. The first white people who settled here didn't name this place Snake Bite Key for nothin'. They had the good sense to leave these parts quick and move on over towards New Orleans where they invented gumbo and jazz and left this ground to Mr. No Shoulders, gators, scorpions, and skeeters."

Willett poured himself another glass of scotch and wet his whistle. The storm outside raged on, and Balls was tuned to the story like a radio. "Now we ain't talkin' normal skeeters 'round these parts. We be talkin' birds with teeth. Well, the swamp stayed like that for a long, long time, and then one day, along comes the craziest white man I ever laid eyes on. The Reverend Sonny Boy Seymour, pastor of the Snake Bite Church of the Righteous Serpent.

"Now rumor had it Reverend Sonny Boy had been

a real waterfront badass and womanizer 'round Mobile. He was a boxer by trade, and his fightin' name was the 'Pascagoula Panther.' He was mean. He'd just knock motherfuckers into next week in the ring. Then he'd pick up his pay and go whorin' 'round Water Street till he spent all his money, and then he'd go back to fightin'. Well, one night on a full moon, it seems Sonny Boy got all liquored up and broke into the drugstore looking for paregoric and grabbed a bottle of lye instead and drank it down. They took him to the hospital and pronounced him dead as a doorknob, and they was rollin' him to the morgue when he woke up spoutin' religion.

"Now we ain't talkin' no holy communion or holy rollin' religion. Sonny Boy was a snake handlin' preacher, and he took to this swamp to start his church in the backyard of the devil himself. He soon got a big followin' of people that didn't have much else to look forward to in life, and he and his disciples would cart drunks off of Water Street and into the swamps for rebirthin'. They would hoot and holler and roll all 'round up there at the church they built out of an old school bus, and they'd run through the swamp catchin' snakes.

"Don't you know *nobody* fucked with Reverend Sonny Boy and his followers. Snake Bite Key was his domain sorta like old Jean Laffite over in Louisiana.

"One day, my cousin Bubba and me was out pullin' crab traps, and Bubba pulls one up. Wound around inside the trap is the biggest goddamn Mr. No Shoulders I ever seen. Ten feet long and a head on him the size of a steam iron. I thought we had caught ourselves a fuckin' sea monster.

"Me and Bubba didn't even think of tryin' to get him

out of the trap. We just hauled him up to Reverend Sonny Boy, 'cause we knew he would pay good money for that snake. We found him asleep in a hammock under the big oak, but he must have sensed somethin', 'cause when we got close, he sprang out of that hammock like he was risin' from the dead again. He saw that Mr. No Shoulders in the crab trap and went berserk, yellin' 'bout how he was lookin' at the devil himself in a chicken-wire prison.

"He started yellin' for all his junior snake handlers to gather 'round the crab trap. That big-ass, mean Mr. No Shoulders just lay there in a ball. The congregation worked itself into an uproar, and Bubba and me got scared as shit when we seen 'em bring out ropes. We lit out of there.

"Late that night, me and Bubba snuck back up there to see what was goin' on, and the snake handlers were gathered 'round a big fire near the school-bus church. We snuck up a good ways on the sandbar behind the church, and it was somethin' to see. Reverend Sonny Boy's getup made him look like the Mardi Gras king. There were beads, buttons, and feathers all over him and snakes hangin' all off of him.

"The congregation stopped singin' and hollerin' when Reverend Sonny Boy raised his hands. He went over to the crab trap and grabbed hold, screamin' for the devil himself to show. He opened the door, and that big old snake rolled out of that trap as slow and dangerous as hot lava headin' for the ocean.

"Reverend Sonny Boy got down on his knees, face-to-face with that snake, and the starin' contest began. They sat there eye-to-eye for hours, and a storm began to roll in from the Gulf. The wind started blowin' a hurricane, and hail as big as golf balls bounced around the ground, and then a blindin' flash of lightnin' hit the school-bus church and melted it down to the size of a coffee table.

"Reverend Sonny Boy saw this and grabbed that snake by its head and commenced to damn him to hell. Well, it may have been the devil or just a big-ass Mr. No Shoulders. But that snake slipped the grip of Sonny Boy, and in midair, he whipped around and struck Sonny Boy in the middle of his head and shot him through the air like a bottle rocket, and Sonny Boy landed on the scrap-metal coffee table that used to be the church.

"Reverend Sonny Boy got up and went for the snake. Blood was pourin' out of two nail-size holes in his head, and his eyes was a-glowin' bright red like Godzilla. Well, they fought and rolled 'round, and then Sonny Boy bit the snake in the middle of its head, and it died dead on the spot. He picked up that snake, tossed him over his shoulder, and walked off into the swamp. He's still around. This is *his* territory, least what's left of it since the golf course got built. And that's the story."

The bottle of scotch had long since disappeared, and the storm outside had gotten worse. Sheets of rain slammed against the big picture window.

"Willett, that's a goddamn fantastic story. I mean, personally, I think you should go on 'Star Search' and tell that one to Ed McMahon. But what does that have to do with the sixteenth hole?"

Willett let out a soft belly laugh and ran his index finger around the inside of his glass and licked it.

" 'Cause the green of number sixteen sits on top of the spot where Reverend Sonny Boy's church melted."

"Does this mean that number sixteen, the hole I just bet Lard Ass Louis Huckle five thousand dollars on, has a mojo on it?"

"That be the correct terminology, Balls."

The storm had not let up at all when Balls staggered outside and jumped into his golf cart. Needless to say, his equilibrium was a bit out of whack. He went right across his cart on the first attempt.

"Don't worry 'bout it, Balls," Willett hollered through the window of his pickup truck. "Who knows? Tomorrow might be your lucky day. Thanks for the drink!"

Willett drove off, and Balls pulled his parka tight over his head. He held a go-cup in one hand and steered with the other. He was wondering if he should believe all that Sonny Boy shit or not when he missed the turn to his house. His wife was away at a cosmetic surgery clinic, and his daughters were away at school, so at least he didn't have to face anyone at home. But when his wife returned and heard about this bet from the biddies at the bridge club, she would kill him.

Tonight Balls just laughed as good scotch traveled through his system, and he thought he ought to just keep driving the golf cart south, gathering speed until he crashed through the barricade at the end of U.S. 1 in Snake Bite Key. He would dive away from the sinking cart, clubs, and golf balls. He would swim and swim until he washed up on the island of Margaritaville where a large-breasted island beauty would revive him with coconut water. And then, of course, they would live happily ever after.

Balls was jolted back to the reality of Snake Bite Key

when a huge limb from an oak tree crashed to the ground in front of him, blocking the path of his cart.

He swerved to the left, and his parka slid up and covered his eyes as the golf cart hydroplaned, did a three-sixty, and collided with a small pine tree. Balls pulled the rain hood off his head. He was completely disoriented. It was pouring and pitch black except for an occasional flash of lightning. He still held the go-cup in one hand. He hadn't spilled a drop.

Balls drained the cup and stepped on the accelerator, and the little cart came to life. He slowly crept along, hoping to find a landmark he would recognize.

Another flash of lightning revealed a cart path on the other side of a long fairway, and Balls aimed his machine in that direction. He thought he knew where he was. Then it happened.

A pair of glowing red eyes was directly in front of him, and when the lightning flashed, Balls saw a huge man standing between him and the cart path. Balls screeched to a halt and slid sideways. Then he cranked up the cart and turned in the opposite direction.

Goose pimples were running up and down his body. The red eyes were in front of him again. Balls stopped and yelled at the glowing red eyes.

"Okay, Lard Ass, if this is your idea of a joke, I don't think it's funny anymore. Just tell me where the fuck I am." He felt the cart move and realized somebody was climbing in.

Balls froze like a popsicle when he saw the red eyes next to him in the cart.

"My name ain't Lard Ass. 'Round these here parts, people call me the Swamp Creature."

The reincarnated Reverend Sonny Boy Seymour was

not your typical creature. He was dressed in a familiar pink-and-green Izod alligator golf shirt and an equally familiar pair of handprinted pants covered with little red lobsters. They were cut off below the knee. He was completely bald—which accentuated the two holes in the middle of his forehead and his big red eyes. At the moment they were staring directly at the rigid figure of Balls Rawls.

"I know you. You're the left-hander who plays with the fat guy who drives the little Rolls-Royce. You've never even hit the green on number sixteen, have ya?"

Balls showed the first evidence that he was still mobile. He slowly turned his head back and forth.

"You need to line up on the water fountain to the left."

A bolt of lightning struck the earth ten feet from Balls's cart and lit the Swamp Creature like a Christmas tree. When the sky turned dark again, Mother Nature had created a big supply of much-needed ozone and left the golf cart glowing with Saint Elmo's fire.

The creature was gone. Balls flew out of the golf cart as if he'd been ejected from a crippled jet and fled as fast as he could from the still-glowing cart. He turned to see if he was being followed and ran full speed into a pecan tree.

Balls was in that limbo of consciousness where he wasn't sure if he was still on the planet or not. "First of all," he wondered, "am I still alive?" He gave himself a test. He stuck his finger in his mouth and bit down hard. It hurt. He *was* still alive. A lone mosquito hovered above his wrist. He watched it land and plug in for a little refreshment. Balls made no attempt to squash the insect. He just let it fill up, and then he watched the mosquito lift off. It spun around and flew directly onto the ground.

"Jesus Christ," Balls muttered, "God only knows what I've got running through my veins today."

He slowly got to his feet. The storm had passed, and it was actually a bit cool. He felt the left side of his face and realized it was one big strawberry from his collision with the pecan tree. Then he saw his banged-up golf cart stuck in the mud. What he had hoped was just a bad dream had, in fact, happened. A shiver went down his spine.

He stumbled back to the cart and saw something on the seat—a small snakeskin bag. He opened it and found a golf ball inside. It was the worst-looking, discolored, cut-up golf ball he had ever seen.

"What the hell happened to you?" Balls started at the sound of the voice. It was Willett.

"Willett, I got to talk to you. I just saw the Swamp Creature, and he was dressed just like Lard Ass."

"Ain't nobody seen the Swamp Creature 'round here in a long time, and besides, you got to remember that there's a lot of truth in a full bottle of whiskey, but a head full of lies in an empty one. That scotch got me goin' pretty good," Willett chuckled.

"But Willett, he was here in the golf cart. Look! He left this." Balls held out the snakeskin bag, and Willett opened it and looked inside at the golf ball.

"You hold on to this. I'll get your clubs," Willett said. He took Balls's golf bag off the cart and loaded it on his shoulder. He took out a seven iron and handed it to Balls. "Double the bet," he said.

* * *

Lard Ass Louis Huckle was the matador of the morning. He was out to humiliate a bad left-handed golfer, a man he didn't really care for anyway, and he was dressed for his mission. He wore a brand-new pair of polyester Key-lime green golf slacks and a matching shirt. All his favorite outfits had been mysteriously disappearing from the clothesline in back of his house, and he couldn't figure out where they were going—especially after his maid passed the lie detector test.

He was in great spirits and had spent an hour at the practice range polishing the seven-iron shot that was going to win him a bundle of money.

He parked his yellow golf cart by the ball washer on the sixteenth tee and watched in amazement as Willett and Balls approached.

"Hey, Balls, you look like you been shot at and missed, and shit at and hit, but a bet is a bet."

"You've got the honors, Lard Ass," Balls said calmly.

"Well, thank you." Lard Ass wasn't quite sure what to make of Balls and his appearance, but he sensed he should leave well enough alone and concentrate on his shot. He knelt down to tee up.

"Bet's doubled," Balls said.

Lard Ass nearly toppled over but came up to look closely at Balls.

"Are you still drunk?" he snorted.

"That may be. . . . Do we have a bet or not? Ten grand. Winner take all."

"You've got a bet, asshole," Lard Ass growled. He looked down the fairway at the flag collapsed against the pin. This was just a straight shot. He got ready to swing.

Good shots are heard before they are seen, and Lard

Ass's shot certainly sounded impressive. The ball gained altitude quickly and then began to fall as if it had been dropped out of the sky. It landed four feet from the pin and gingerly rolled another two feet toward the hole. Lard Ass didn't say a word. He just gestured to Balls to take the tee.

Willett handed Balls the funky old golf ball from the glowing cart. Balls teed it up, looked down the fairway, and lined himself up with the water fountain way to the left of the green. Lard Ass watched in silence as Balls got ready to hit.

Willett, staring off into the woods at the left, saw a pair of red eyes glowing through the morning mist. "Oh, my God," he gasped.

Balls looked down at the old ball, and without hesitating or thinking, he swung. The ball went out over the water to the right like it always did, and Louis started to cheer.

Suddenly the flag on the pinstick snapped straight out to the left, and a huge gust of wind blew the ball back toward the green. It hit dead in the center of the hole, rattling the pin as it settled.

Lard Ass fainted on the spot, and Willett just stood there. His mouth dropped open, and then he began to howl.

"Damn, Willett, you act like you've never seen a hole in one before," Balls said calmly. Then he started screaming with joy. The two men hugged each other and rolled around on the ground just like they did years before in the muddy end zone after beating Bundy High.

Balls rolled over on top of Lard Ass and stuck his hand into a polyester pocket and pulled out a roll of hundred-dollar bills. He counted five thousand dollars and handed it to Willett. "Thanks for the tip. I'm gonna sit here and wait for Lard Ass to wake up and write me a check for the rest."

"Well, if you don't mind, I'd like to sit here and wait with you."

"That's fine with me," Balls snickered, and they just took up laughing and howling again.

Meanwhile, on the other side of the man-made lake on hole sixteen of the Soft Shell Golf and Country Club in the town of Heat Wave on Snake Bite Key in the state of Alabama in the U.S.A. on the planet Earth near the close of the twentieth century, only the water moccasins heard the sound of a single pair of hands clapping.

The Swamp Creature had let one in.

THE PASCAGOULA RUN

Jim Delaney heard the telephone ring and climbed out from under the covers. He was on his feet but still half asleep as he ran to the phone. When he picked up the receiver he was awake enough to realize the room temperature was just above freezing.

"James Delaney, this is your grandmother. I want to make sure you don't miss the train. Your cousins from New York will be here for just two days and are dying to see you. You *are* coming, aren't you?" she demanded.

"Yes, ma'am, but it sure is cold," he said. His teeth chattered.

"It's brisk, young man, but the cold air is good for your circulation. Now, regarding your cousins—they only come here once a year, and we have to be hospitable to them. That's the southern way."

Jim was trying to stretch the phone cord far enough

across the room to get to his clothes. They were draped over the warm coils of the radiator.

"Call when you get to the station, and I'll come get you. Bye, love."

"Okay, Grandma," he said and hung up the phone. "Damn Yankees!" he shouted. He had never liked those cousins. All they did was talk about who won the Civil War.

He had been working for his father on weekends in the boatyard and had successfully avoided seeing his relatives this time. But Grandma was set on a rendezvous.

Jim grabbed his clothes and ran back to bed. He dressed under the warm patchwork quilt, and he rolled out onto the floor. It was unusually quiet in the old creole house. On a workday it would have been a beehive of activity: his father and the workmen from the family boatyard next door always began the day with coffee and shipyard talk. But this Saturday he was alone. His father had gone south to pick up a boat and had taken his mother with him.

Jim did *not* want to go to Pascagoula, but if he had thoughts of canceling, he'd have to call back soon and have a real good excuse. Bingo, his old chow dog, crawled out from under the bed and stretched halfway across the room. The dog's breath frosted over.

"Come on, Bingo," Jim called.

He wiped the moisture off a windowpane. It was still dark outside, and the boats in the yard sat in various states of repair under a blanket of frost. Out on the porch the big Barq's Root Beer thermometer read thirty-one degrees.

The swirling layer of fog that covered the surface of

the inlet reminded him of scenes from horror movies. He thought of the local legend about the Swamp Creature of Snake Bite Key. He shivered, but not from fear.

In the kitchen he lit paper under a pile of wood in the small fireplace, and quickly the blaze began to warm the air. He heated a pan of milk and made hot chocolate, sipping it carefully so it wouldn't scald his tongue.

Jim had watched this cold front draw closer and closer to the Gulf Coast. A marvelous new satellite sent pictures of the whole country's weather patterns back to earth in seconds, and the local weatherman on the Pensacola TV station was like a kid with a new toy—he finally had something important to trace with his pointer. Astronauts were blasting off for outer space from a small peninsula on the Atlantic coast of Florida. This was an exciting time to be alive. The world was becoming smaller, and Jim wanted to see it all.

He called the train station, and, to his delight, the train was running an hour late. He phoned his grandmother.

"Don't sound so happy," she said. "If the train is too late, your Uncle Raymond will come over and get you. They are just *dying* to see you."

Now he was worse off than before. Two hours in a car with Curt and Burt was more than he could take.

"Grandma still thinks I'm about eight years old," he told Bingo. "Last Christmas she gave me a water pistol. And she refuses to believe I have a driver's license. Why would I want to hang out with two twelve-year-olds?" Facing a hopeless battle, he went back to the kitchen and made some more hot chocolate. While the milk was heating up, he sat by the fire and thumbed through the latest copy of *National Geographic*. The photographs took him far away from Snake Bite Key.

Jim Delaney had been reading *National Geographic* for a long time and had compiled two journals of notes on the places he was going to visit. A two-page picture of a huge fort rising above a tropical jungle filled him with longing. The article told the story of a black king who helped defeat Napoleon's troops and liberate Saint-Domingue—as Haiti was called in those days. The king built an unbelievable fortress that some said was the equal of the pyramids. It was called the Citadel.

The article included photographs of old cannons and thousands of cannonballs strewn around the interior of the fortress. There seemed to be no guards or tour guides keeping a strict eye on the place the way they did at Fort Morgan. Jim and his friends had been chased away from the manicured powder magazines more times than he could remember. No, the only guards in the pictures were smiling locals who smoked unfiltered cigarettes and drank beer from brown bottles.

He finished the article, glanced again at his watch, and called for Bingo. Both of them went out into the icy morning. There were two hours before the ferry left for the train station. A thundering noise came from out over the water. He searched the sky for the source of the sound and spotted a bright reflection just above the surface of the bay. Then they soared out of the sun, six F11F Tigers in close formation. In a few seconds they were overhead with a deafening roar. The Blue Angels flew in so low they kicked up rooster tails of spray on the surface of the bay before shooting straight back up into the sun.

This makes getting up early worthwhile, Jim thought.

The sun had melted the morning frost, and the earth was beginning to warm up. He stretched out on the dock and decided to call his grandmother to tell her he wasn't coming. Spellbound, he watched the entire Blue Angel practice. He could see himself in the cockpit of one of the fighters, straining against the g forces, pulling his plane into a steep bank over the shoreline above the Florida-Alabama border. If you have to have a real job, he thought, this wouldn't be a bad one.

Jim was lost in the sky and didn't hear the sports car screech up his driveway. He also didn't see the big man hoist himself out of the car. What he *did* feel was confusion when a huge shadow above him blocked out the sun.

"Goddamn federal-subsidized motorcycle gang!" the man bellowed.

Jim Delaney leaped straight to his feet like a springer spaniel. The man on the dock was looking skyward toward the vanishing planes.

"Uncle Billy!" Jim shouted. "Where did you come from?"

"Yesterday I was in Miami, the day before, Rio. How's that for starters?"

Billy Delaney was larger than life. Jim's father's six-foot-six black sheep of a younger brother had fought among a stable of young fighters sponsored by a local brewery. He had also been such a tenacious tailback he was almost guaranteed a scholarship to Ole Miss, but when the Japanese bombed Pearl Harbor, Billy's life—like a lot of others in that era—took another turn.

He lied about his age and joined the Navy, then went to the Pacific where he fought Japs, and won medals for bravery. He survived the sinking of his PT boat and married a Tahitian princess for five days.

After the war Billy went to work for a steamship company in Hong Kong. When he made it to first mate he kept the position for nearly twenty-five years; the responsibilities of captain would have limited his freedom. He circled the globe like a satellite and had the scars and tattoos to prove it. Young Jim had received presents from the far corners of the world since he was a baby.

"Them goddamn Navy fly-boys always thought they were hot shit, but the surface Navy is the *Navy*. Ships were here long before planes, and they'll be here a long time after every plane falls out of the sky. Where's your mom and dad?"

"They took a boat to Cedar Key and won't be back till Monday."

"So what are you doing?"

"The Yankees are in Pascagoula, and Grandma ordered me to come down and play the Delaney southern hospitality game. My train is late, and if it gets later, Uncle Raymond is going to come get me. Are you on your way home to Grandma's?"

"Yeah, but this sure puts a different light on the subject. I'm not ready for Raymond's 'when are you going to get your life together' speech. I'll take you to Pascagoula, and if we get cornered, they're easier to take when you're not alone. Come on, I want to show you something."

Jim followed close behind Billy, and his mouth dropped open when he saw the red Jaguar XKE convertible shimmering in the morning sun. Jim Delaney ran his hand across the left fender and walked all the way around the car. He let out a long, slow whistle. Here in his own driveway was the beautiful machine he had only seen in car magazines. Nothing on earth smelled like genuine leather seats, and he was amazed by the fancy new eight-track car stereo unit.

"It's not stolen, just the fruits of hard labor from years of stompin' spiders on banana boats. Here," Billy said, tossing the keys to Jim, "you're now my driver. Let's go face our dragons, shall we?"

Jim just couldn't believe it. Talk about good reasons to get up early! He slid into the driver's seat and revved up the V-12 engine. The tachometer needle rose and fell. He eased off on the clutch and hit the accelerator and let out a wild yell. Billy hollered even louder. They were off on the "Pascagoula Run."

Jim Delaney was in heaven. His nose was running, and tears streamed out of his eyes behind his Polaroid sunglasses as he sped along Highway 59 toward Gulf Shores. The cold morning air had no effect on him; he raced up the bridge across Perdido inlet and looked out over the entire Gulf Coast of Alabama. The stereo system was cranked up to the max. Fats Domino sang "Walking to New Orleans," as Billy and Jim sang along.

None of Jim's other uncles had even heard of Fats Domino, but Billy knew a little about everything. Jim's father had always talked about how crazy his younger brother was, but Jim could tell that deep down his father truly loved his younger brother for just being himself. They stopped in Gulf Shores to call his grandmother to tell her they were on the way.

"What did she say?" Jim asked when Billy came back from the booth.

" 'Don't be late.' "

At the only stoplight in town a carload of young teenage girls pulled up beside the Jaguar and squealed at the sight of the car.

Then, to their shock, they saw that Jim was the driver, and they began screaming for him to take them for a ride.

"This here car's makin' their little adolescent nipples hard, you can count on that. Come on, pull over," Billy said. He waved for the carload of girls to follow. Billy went to the Pak A Sak and bought a six-pack of Jax and sipped away while Jim took each of the girls for a spin and then introduced them all to his uncle. Duly impressed, the girls all piled back into their Mustang fastback.

Billy got back in the car. "Young Jim," he said, "stick with me, and you'll get more girls than Frank Sinatra."

They were in the middle of eating an oyster loaf at Mack's Cafe in Battles Wharf when Jim Delaney was overcome by his sense of responsibility—or the lack of it. "Oh my God," he cried out, "I forgot to feed Bingo, and I left the house unlocked, and . . ."

"Whoa," Billy said, holding his hands up like a traffic cop. "You're having a very bad attack of Catholic guilt there. Let me ask you something. You think Bingo is going to go hungry in a day? And when is the last time you ever locked your house? I know this is all new to you, Young Jim, but I've been at it for quite a while. I don't want to be a bad influence, but it's about time you had a little fun. And besides, you can blame me for everything. Now, eat your oyster loaf before it gets cold. This is the best oyster loaf in the world, and I've traveled damn near six thousand miles to eat here, and we got a few more stops to make before we get to Grandma's house.''

Jim gulped down his root beer while Billy paid the check and had a quick flirt with the waitress. They were walking out to the car when Billy took a pint of rum from the pocket of his black leather jacket and took a swig.

''Don't get any ideas, junior,'' he said, looking at Jim. ''You got plenty of time to make up for lost time.''

''How come you still live at Grandma's so much?'' Jim asked.

'' 'Cause I've never been on land long enough to think about having a place of my own. Besides, I liked my room as a kid, and I still like it as a man. But I would've stayed where I was if I'd have known Raymond was visiting.''

''Grandma says that you just won't grow up,'' Jim said.

''Do you think that's bad?'' Billy asked.

''Not at all.''

They drove north to Spanish Fort and around the big oval onto Highway 90. They both looked out at the rotting frame of the old ship that lay dying in the tidal pool. It was still quite cold, but they kept the top down. In the Bankhead Tunnel Jim blew the horn, and the guards blew their whistles. Now Jim was getting the feel of the Jag; he downshifted and shot out of the tunnel like a watermelon seed. They cruised under the oak trees lining Government Street and were soon out of town, heading west, as the winter sun set off early toward New Orleans.

"Keep her on the road, sport. I'm gonna grab a little combat nap." Billy dozed off in seconds.

Jim tuned the radio to WTIX in the French Quarter and listened to Aaron Neville singing "Tell It Like It Is." He finally pulled off the road near Grand Bay and put the white top up. It was already dark and getting colder, and it wasn't worth freezing when nobody could even see them.

In the distance a cluster of neon lights marked the state line between Alabama and Mississippi. Jim had heard of the notorious stateline bars from his friends in school. The drinking age in Mississippi was eighteen, and they made fake IDs from driver's license renewal forms.

These were the wild places that catered to the waterfront crowd from Pascagoula and the paper mill workers from Moss Point. Jim often traveled this road to visit his grandmother, and he had always wondered what really went on inside those cheap frame buildings. Just then Billy popped awake, as clear as if he had slept all night.

"Pull into the Oasis, Young Jim. It's cocktail hour."

"I better call Grandma and tell her we might be late."

"I think she already knows."

Jim weaved through the parking lot full of pickup trucks until he found a spot. The second he stopped the car, Billy was out and running. He marched through the battered front door and announced his presence to a packed house by shouting, "Hide the women, and pour the whiskey! Billy Delaney's back in port!"

He was greeted by a wild group of well-wishers who lifted him up onto their shoulders and carried him to the bar. Before Jim knew it, he, too, was hoisted above the crowd and carried inside. From his strange vantage point, Jim looked down on a first-class honky-tonk.

The big, smoke-filled room was jammed with boisterous partying people. In one corner a drunken man was being dragged out the door by his hair. The bouncers were two enormous men with more tattoos than Jim had ever seen. A red-headed woman in a tight dress flipped the bird at the man when he was finally jerked out the door. It took a minute for Jim to realize that one of the bouncers was the popular local wrestling villain Crab Man Dan who was famous for beating his good-looking opponents into submission with a crab trap every other Saturday night at the National Guard armory in Foley.

Billy stood on the bar and bellowed what an honor it was to be back in his home state. A bevy of painted office girls from the nearby paper mill clapped and cheered. He introduced his nephew, and the girls studied Jim Delaney's young frame up on the bar and chewed their gum faster. Mugs of draft beer were sent their way, and after watching his uncle guzzle one down, Jim emulated his every move.

He spent an undetermined amount of time on the small dance floor with the paper mill girls and was sandwiched between a pair of identical twins in stretch pants who tried to make a po' boy sandwich out of him. They marched around the room while the combo behind the chicken wire on the bandstand sang a hot rendition of "The Battle of New Orleans."

Jim Delaney was happily smothered by wire bras and soft breasts and had already promised to drive the twins home in the Jaguar. A wave of guilt swept over him.

He was having too much fun, and his grandmother was going to kill him. He would have to go to confession real soon.

Suddenly screams, crashing, and the sound of broken glass sent bodies climbing over bodies, and the dance floor emptied. A man brandishing a chain saw ripped through the crowd. Jim recognized him—he was the man thrown out earlier.

Jim Delaney knew he was going to die. The beer-soaked boards beneath his feet would give way, and he would fall straight into the fires of hell.

But in a flash, Billy was at his side. "Let's get out of here. Things are getting too bizarre."

The man with the chain saw was *not* in a cheerful mood. His face was cut, and his nose was as flat as a deboned chicken breast. He was carving up tables and chairs, and the terrifying whine of the saw echoed through the room. Then he saw Crab Man Dan by the door. In less than a minute Mr. Chain Saw had Crab Man Dan pinned in the corner and was closing in, jabbing at him with the saw.

"You don't look so tough now, motherfucker!" Mr. Chain Saw screamed above the roar of the saw.

Four men were trying to get behind him, and one held a chair over his head, but Mr. Chain Saw either sensed or saw them, and he turned and cut the chair in two. The men leaped back into the crowd.

Again, Mr. Chain Saw focused his venomous grin on Crab Man Dan. The tattooed wrestler fell to his knees and begged for mercy.

"I don't think he's faking this," Jim said to the frightened paper mill twins. Meanwhile, Mr. Chain Saw just laughed louder, taunting the big man on his knees.

He started toward the Crab Man, but precisely then his moment of glory came to an end.

The saw engine sputtered, coughed, and ran out of gas. Crab Man Dan came to his senses and jerked the man and his chain saw high over his head and catapulted both through the painted window near the back door.

Wailing sirens and flashing lights of the Mississippi highway patrol poured into the parking lot of the Oasis as Billy Delaney eased the red Jag back onto the highway. He looked over at his nephew, who now resembled Mrs. Lot after she had been turned into a pillar of salt.

"I don't suppose you want to check out the twins over in Moss Point, do ya?" Billy asked. He belched and let out a yelp. He was ready to party.

Jim turned and stared at his uncle in disbelief. "You've got to be kidding, Uncle Billy," he pleaded.

"It's amazing how a little adrenaline rush can straighten you right up. Remember that," Billy said. The Jag sped along smoothly, and he began to laugh.

Jim relaxed and finally started laughing too, and they ended up whooping and screaming all the way to Pascagoula.

Shortly before sunrise they pulled onto Beach Road and quietly drove up to the old family house. The full moon lit up the driveway, and Billy quietly drove the Jag in, coasting the last fifty yards. They tiptoed into the old house and silently stepped across the kitchen floor. Just then the big oak door swung open. Grandma stood there. Jim Delaney froze. Now he *knew* he was going to die.

"Hi, Mom," Billy said brightly. He walked right over

and kissed her. "Hope we didn't wake you when we came in last night. Thought we'd get up early. We were just on our way to fish the turn of the tide down at the Coast Guard base before church."

"No, you didn't wake me up," Grandma said. "We've had so much excitement 'round here with Burt and Curt and Raymond that we were all tired out. I meant to wait up for you boys, but we had us *such* a big time yesterday. And today'll be even busier with y'all here."

"Well, tell Raymond we'll be back in two hours, and we're dying to see him." Billy looked at Jim and winked. "We'll pick up the bait down at Hatcher's."

"See you in a little while, Grandma," Jim said and followed his uncle out the door.

"Guess we're goin' fishin', like it or not, Young Jim." Billy's eyes were red as roses, and fishing was clearly the last thing on earth he wanted to do.

"Guess so," Jim sighed. "You think Grandma bought it? What's she gonna do when she sees we haven't slept in our beds?" They were almost to the water. The temperature had plummeted, and Jim could see his breath freeze over.

"I've been makin' my bed as neat as can be since my first week in the Navy. Let's just say I'm a good influence and taught you to do the same."

They sat on the windy pilings by the Coast Guard base freezing their butts off. Their fishing lines hung slack in the water. Every five minutes or so they looked at their watches, waiting for the two hours to elapse before they could go back to the warm house.

"Uncle Bill, how did you ever learn how to think

that fast?'' Jim asked. His teeth chattered from the cold, and his hands were raw.

''Let's just say it wasn't the first time I've had to resort to a little deception when dealing with your grandmother.'' Billy shivered. ''Damn, it's like the North Pole out here today.''

''I'm so tired. I just want to sleep all day, but instead I'm going to have to go to church, and then I have to spend all day being hospitable to the Yankee brats.''

''Well I guess I forgot to tell you one of the rules about having too much fun. If you play, you have to pay. Don't forget that.''

Just then the slack line on Jim's pole went taut. He had hooked a fish. ''It's a big one!'' Jim hollered, and all at once the exhaustion and cold melted away. A new day had begun in Pascagoula.

I WISH LUNCH COULD LAST FOREVER

Martinique

Isabella was a child of the volcano. She had grown up in the coastal city of Saint-Pierre—a city called the "Paris of the Indies" until Mount Pelée exploded in the early twentieth century and incinerated twenty-nine thousand people and the village. The town drunk, who had been spending the night in jail in an underground cell, was the sole survivor. He eventually joined P. T. Barnum's Greatest Show on Earth.

Eventually Saint-Pierre was built into a town again by surviving relatives of the victims. Isabella lived at the convent on Rue Ursaline where she had been left, as a baby, on the doorstep. She was raised by the nuns, who taught her to speak English and fear for her everlasting soul. Each Saturday morning when Isabella walked to market, she watched the cane cutters out in the fields and overheard conversations in waterfront bars near the Place de Mouillage. She knew she had to do more than live her entire life in the shadow of the volcano.

At night she restlessly walked the black beaches, staring out over the sea at the distant running lights of ships passing in the lee of the island. She knew such a boat would someday take her away to see the world.

Under her mosquito net, in the tropical morning air, Isabella lay dreaming. She was high in the rigging of a beautiful schooner, looking down at the world below. She sailed over the mouth of the volcano and peered down into the glowing embers. There she saw the faces of her dead parents; they told her not to come too close to the volcano or she would be robbed of her youth. Then she was on the Mississippi River talking with the legendary explorer Iberville, who spoke to her about his city: New Orleans. A flock of shorebirds flew around her and sang haunting songs she had never heard before.

She woke briefly and stared out at a night rainbow over the water. Then she closed her eyes tight and eventually found her way back to the dream—but now she was in Paris. She stood in front of a mirror and watched herself change from a beautiful young girl into an older woman.

Isabella woke again to a cloud of hummingbirds flurrying around her bed. She went to the window. There in the moonlight, the ship of her dreams lay at anchor in the harbor. A large American flag flew from the stern. After she pinched herself to make sure this was not a dream, she smiled and set about packing her few possessions into a cardboard suitcase. It was her eighteenth birthday.

At work that day she went through the motions of caring about her job—listening to the honored lunch guest, a priest who ranted on and on about saving immortal souls. She peeked through the kitchen windows at the harbor below where the boat was at anchor.

That afternoon Isabella left the plantation and walked to town. She sat on the black beach and stared, transfixed, out at the majestic ship in the calm waters of the bay.

Finally, a small boat was lowered. A tall man in faded khakis pulled the dinghy up to the shore and almost tripped over a huge shark that some fisherman had dragged onto the beach to butcher. The blond stranger was talking to one of the Creole planters, and they laughed and hugged each other. Meanwhile, a large oak barrel of rum was rolled through the sand and into the dinghy.

Impulsively, Isabella ran to the beach to help the stranger shove his boat back into the water, and he almost fell overboard from the tippy dinghy when he saw the beautiful young girl next to the boat; in the clear water her long, print skirt clung to her perfectly shaped legs. He introduced himself as Captain Will from Nantucket. He thanked her in French and offered to show her his ship when he returned to town later that evening. Isabella waited in the square and wrote a long letter to Mother Superior.

That evening Captain Will rowed Isabella out to the schooner. She loved the smell of the old boat and felt a security she had never felt before. She stepped barefoot onto the deck of the *Basil M. Gelder*, listening to the captain's tales of his own life and those of the boat. Finally she looked up at the shore, and for the first time saw her whole little world from a distance. She could see the town with its ruins scattered between the new buildings, and above the town expansive green fields seemed to move as ribbons of cane swayed in the breeze. Towering over it all was the ever-present volcano. She was frightened at how tiny the village of Saint-Pierre looked lying in the shadow of the volcano.

Captain Will took her back to shore and told her he was sailing for Trinidad in the morning. He kissed her on the lips and said good-bye.

Isabella returned to her grandmother's house and taped the letter she had written to the door. She had tried hard to explain her departure from Martinique. She retrieved her bag from its hiding place behind the giant y'lang-y'lang tree and wandered through the streets of Saint-Pierre all night, breathing in the mixture of fragrant tropical flowers and kitchen smells. In front of a bar on Rue de Victor Hugo she stopped and listened to a beguine on the Victrola and watched the people slow dancing so close they seemed glued together. Isabella carefully stored these memories in her mind and walked to the black beach and into the sea. Slowly she swam toward the schooner, holding her suitcase high above her head.

Soaking wet, she climbed into the dinghy and slept there until she was discovered the next morning by one of the crew members. "Captain Will," she announced, "I want to go away on your ship." He was curious and somewhat amused. She was a rumpled mess, but all the more enchanting for it. In the early morning light they drank café au lait, and she told him of her dream.

"Look long and hard at the shore," he said, "for once the anchor is up, we'll be on our way."

At Sea

Captain Will and Isabella sailed the Caribbean happily for nearly two years. Isabella became quite a sailor, rarely sleeping below deck. She preferred the tranquillity of a hammock beneath the stars.

One night as she lay next to Captain Will, she dreamed of birds and music far away in the city of New Orleans, and one of the birds turned into a man. When Isabella woke the next morning, she knew in her heart it was time to move on. Gently she told Captain Will of her intentions to pursue her dream.

"Come with me," she begged.

"Isabella, you know I love you very much, but the sea and my ship are my life. Besides, this is *your* dream. I have to follow my own."

The idea of separating was sad and difficult, but Isabella had made up her mind. Captain Will maintained his sense of humor through it all, and he gave Isabella two parting gifts: U.S. citizenship from a hastily arranged marriage and divorce, and the ship's clock. He jokingly said the clock would come in handy now that she had decided to go ashore and spend some time on the beach—where clocks were more a part of life's routine than they were on the open sea.

They sailed from St. Barts to San Juan. There she took a steamer to New Orleans, and as the big ship pulled out of San Juan harbor, she stood on the fantail and watched the *Basil M. Gelder*, with Captain Will at the helm, disappear over the horizon. He was sailing off to the Antilles, to the island where she had been born and raised. Staring out at the sea, she felt great anguish for the loss of Captain Will. Aboard the *Basil M. Gelder* she had been able to return to Martinique often, but now there seemed to be no reason. Isabella knew one chapter of her life was over and another unwritten one was about to begin. She trusted her heart to show her the way.

New Orleans

Isabella arrived in New Orleans with a good grasp of English, a little French money, and the clock. She was soon established in an apartment and working for Madame Le Fort, an old lady from Tours who made dolls in a small shop on Rue Royal.

After her long day at work Isabella would stop by the Napoleon House for an aperitif and a sandwich and then follow the sound of jazz into a little bistro on Toulouse Street. Her nights were filled with music by a piano player named Slade Patterson with whom she fell in love on a Sunday afternoon at a lunch that would last forever.

It was in the French Market in New Orleans that she first talked to Slade Patterson. So many times she had seen him from the back of the bistro and listened to him play, through the spectacle of the audience—diehard jazz freaks, off-work bartenders, strippers, and drunk conventioneers from tiny southern towns. But now, in the French Market, Slade sat in the Morning Call at a quiet corner table, free from cigarette smoke and stage lights. He was reading the *Sunday Times-Picayune*.

"You have a suntan!" Isabella exclaimed. And then she could not believe she had said it.

Slade Patterson lay down the paper and looked up at the flustered young woman who stood beside him.

"Thank you very much," he said. "Would you care to sit down and examine it closer?"

Isabella sat and apologized a thousand times. "I love your music."

"I saw you the first day you came into the club, and I asked around to find out who the beautiful girl in the corner was, but no one knew."

Isabella told him about her life in Saint-Pierre and her adventures with Captain Will. Slade listened closely. "Do you eat lunch?" he asked.

They walked over to Galatoire's where they ate gumbo and crawfish salad. Then Slade told her about himself.

"I grew up on a small island off the coast of Alabama called Snake Bite Key. All my family had been fishermen. I worked on the boats till I was about seventeen. I thought that was what I would do with my life until one night, in a waterfront bar in Port Aransas, Texas, I watched a local piano player at work. I immediately knew that was what I wanted to do. The piano player's name was Billy Voltaire, and he came from Miami.

"I talked to Billy on the break and held out five twenty-dollar bills and told him I wanted to take piano lessons. We stayed up all night, and by the time I got back to the boat at sunrise, I knew my days at sea were numbered.

"I bought a used piano, and it took over my life. I played like a man possessed. By summertime I was working at a little bar in Texas. I've worked my way across the Gulf Coast in roadhouses and military bases—but I always knew that New Orleans was the place I wanted to be."

Slade sipped a steamy glass of coffee and looked down from the balcony over the French Quarter.

"New Orleans," he said, "is the cradle of eccentrics. To the sons and daughters of the Confederacy in all the hamlets of the South who chose not to follow the traditional path of birth, death, Junior League, and country club, it's the only place to be. New Orleans is a gumbo, a melting pot of food, mood, mud, and blood, where the Caribbean begins or ends, depending on your point of view." He grinned at Isabella. "And it's as close as I can get to Paris. But one day I *will* get to Paris."

Isabella smiled shyly at Slade and raised her glass of coffee. "And so will I."

They were never apart much after that. Isabella moved into Slade's little apartment on Ursuline Street amid a colorful array of neighbors: a warlock, a gay couple, a retired lion tamer, strippers, and a treasure diver.

Every day around noon Slade stopped by the doll shop for their lunchtime rendezvous, and they ate at one of their fifty favorite spots in the French Quarter. Cocktail hour was spent around a fountain in the courtyard of the apartment building. The goldfish swam so slowly you could pick them up, and building gossip was the topic of the day among all the neighbors.

Isabella and Slade rarely ventured out of the Quarter,

but occasionally they rode the St. Charles Avenue streetcar out to see the azaleas in bloom on their way to have a pecan waffle at the Camellia Grill. Once Slade took Isabella to Pontchartrain Beach. They rode a roller coaster called the Zephyr—the highest vantage point in a city below sea level.

Slade was mesmerized by the songs he heard on the few old records Isabella still had from Martinique. He began to weave the melodies and rhythms into his own compositions. Isabella loved listening to the combination of New Orleans jazz and calypso from home, and she introduced Slade to the drink she called "petit punch."

He wrote her a song by that name; he would play, and she would dance the merengue out on the balcony above the night creatures in the streets below.

That year when they went to Mardi Gras, they dressed as life-sized versions of the dolls in Isabella's shop. Madame Le Fort made costumes for them. They stood in the crowds along Canal Street and waved frantically at the participants of the Zulu parade, hoping to catch a glimpse of the Black King of the Mardi Gras. Isabella caught a golden coconut, and they reveled in the streets until the bells of the cathedral rang in Ash Wednesday, announcing the time for repentance.

The next morning Isabella went to work but found the shop locked. She went upstairs to Madame Le Fort's tiny apartment and knocked, but there was no answer. When she opened the door and walked in, she found Madame Le Fort in her bed surrounded by her favorite dolls. She looked as pale and fragile as her porcelain creations.

Madame Le Fort had requested a jazz funeral procession to take her coffin to the ship that would carry her back to France. There she would be buried with her family in Tours. Isabella and Slade led the long line of people through the rainy streets. They tried their best to be as happy as Madame Le Fort wanted them to be, but their sadness at the loss of a friend was very deep.

"She willed the shop to me," Isabella told Slade, "and I don't know what to do. I'm not sure about the responsibility. I'm not sure what to do with the rest of my life."

Isabella began to cry, and Slade gently took her into his arms. She was still sobbing when the boat disappeared around the bend in the river as it turned toward Barataria and the open waters of the Gulf.

"I think it's time we got out of the Quarter for a while," Slade told Isabella. "We're going to Bar-B-Q Hill."

They boarded the *Hummingbird* at the Poydras Street station that afternoon and traveled east through the bayous toward the Gulf Coast. The weather had started to break, and they could feel the funeral cloud passing from above them. The sunny spring day was ushering in something new.

They ate lunch in the dining car. Meanwhile, the train crossed the long bridge at Bay St. Louis, and Isabella was beginning to feel better with the help of a little champagne. Slade had not been home since he had gone off on his fateful trip to Port Aransas, and he was excited.

In Mobile they got off the train and a grand reunion took place between Slade and his younger brother, Kirk. They all climbed into the truck and began the drive south to the beach.

Isabella studied the geography and marveled at how much it looked like parts of Guadeloupe where she used to go with Captain Will. The truck passed marshes, bayous, and roadside stands filled with vegetables and seafood. She knew she was going to like the place where Slade was taking her. They stopped in Bon Secour and had dinner at Meme's, where they dined on fried speckled trout and oyster stew.

Kirk was a quiet man who ran the family boat, now that their father had retired. He asked question after question about Slade's life, and he was obviously taken with Isabella.

"There ain't no middle ground on Snake Bite Key, Isabella," he told her. "You either spend your whole life here, or you get the hell out and see the world. But the ones who stay are just as happy as the ones who go. I don't know too many other places like that. Do you, brother?"

"No I don't, baby brother. I truly don't."

Snake Bite Key

It was dark by the time they drove onto the island across the causeway. Loud, bizarre noises came from the direction of the big swamp. Embers scattered aloft, and the sky glowed from the eerie light of a big bonfire.

"What the hell's going on over there?" Slade asked.

"Snake handlers," Kirk said. "Reverend Sonny Boy is gettin' 'em all riled up, but I hear his days are numbered, 'cause some of the big-money boys from Mobile want to build a golf course out here. Can you imagine that?"

"I'll take the snake handlers any day," Slade said.

They drove to the old Patterson place, and Isabella met Slade's parents, who were waiting up in their pajamas. His mother hugged and kissed them both and wanted them to come in, but Slade said it was late; they would come back in the morning.

Vince Patterson, Slade's father, was clearly a fisherman.

"I raised this kid to fish, but instead he found the piano. Maybe you've finally decided to come home and get a real job," he joked.

"I've been avoiding just that all my life, Daddy," Slade replied.

Slade took the truck and dropped Kirk at the Homeport Bar, and he drove on to the end of the island. He stopped in front of a small frame house atop the biggest sand dune Isabella had ever seen. The whole island was visible from the porch, and a spring breeze from the southwest whistled through the sea oats. Slade held Isabella and kissed her on the nose.

"Welcome to Bar-B-Q Hill," he whispered.

Pink azaleas and white dogwoods covered the island like tiny clouds just above the surface. That first night on Snake Bite Key Isabella took off her shoes, and for two weeks she did not put them back on. She felt like an island girl again. They sailed, swam, fished, and walked the low tides at night carrying a huge mantled light so they could search for soft-shell crabs and flounder.

"It's amazing," Slade remarked, "this place was knocked flat five years ago by a hurricane that cut the island in two, but they built it back."

One afternoon they sailed Kirk's small catboat over to Heat Wave and had dinner at the Northern Lights Cafe. The two sisters who owned the place made a big fuss when they saw Slade again, and they turned the jukebox up and danced a variation of the merengue with Isabella.

The rest of the evening was spent at the Homeport Bar. Isabella introduced the local fishermen to petit punch, and Slade played the old piano until well after dark. They sailed home in the reflection of a full moon, which showed them the way back to Bar-B-Q Hill.

Isabella learned the local recipes from Slade's mother. They were not unlike the spicy dishes of her childhood—"with a little country cookin' thrown in," as Slade put it. He seemed to draw new energy from the little island, and it went directly into his songwriting. He worked from before sunrise until noon, and then they had their traditional lunch together and spent the afternoon on the beach. The days went by much too fast; they always do when you're having fun.

One night Slade and Isabella drove down to the Homeport Bar and sat side by side on the old wooden bench. The owner brought their order of crab cakes and poured a pile of piping hot shrimp on the table. He gave them a roll of paper towels, a bowl of lemons, and a bottle of Crystal hot sauce, and Isabella and Slade discussed their future over a pitcher of beer and a mountain of pink crustaceans.

"I'm going to sell the shop, Slade. It was Madame Le Fort's dream to live in a world of dolls—not mine. I know she would approve of me using what she gave me to make a life for myself. Eventually your music is going to take you away from me," Isabella said softly.

"You know it as well as I do. I don't resent it. Your heart is in your work, and I want you to be happy. I want both of us to be happy. But things are going to change. I've thought about it, and I've decided to go to Paris."

Slade stopped eating. He took her hand. She was not surprised to see tears in his eyes. "I can think of a thousand ways to tell you this is the wrong thing to do."

"Unfortunately it's the *right* thing to do," she said. The ice of the future had been broken.

"I've been offered a record deal by a big company in New York," Slade said. "I didn't know how to tell you before. I was afraid I'd lose you. I know it's not the life you want."

"But it's what *you* want, isn't it?" she asked.

"Oh, yes. But you won't come with me, will you."

"Slade, the dream of records and concerts and tours belongs to you, not to me. I've heard wonderful things about Paris. Remember how we talked of it that first day we had lunch? Remember how much you wanted to go there? I feel something good is waiting there for *me*."

They drove back to the little house on Bar-B-Q Hill and made love until dawn. Slade wept, and Isabella held him until he finally fell asleep. A few hours later they got up and had breakfast with Slade's parents. Then Kirk drove them to Mobile to catch the train back to New Orleans. The tide was low, and the mud flats were exposed in the morning light. A pungent smell filled the air.

"That's the sweet smell of home," Slade said, looking out over the causeway. "I know I can always come home."

"You don't need to come home. You carry it always with you."

The *Hummingbird* pulled into the station in Mobile after its long trek from Cincinnati. The porters and conductors were happy to see the water again and laughed and carried on; they knew they would be home by evening.

Isabella and Slade waved good-bye to Kirk from the window of the train, and they slept in each other's arms the whole way back.

New Orleans

Slade went off to New York with a suitcase full of sheet music and a pocketful of dreams, while Isabella stayed in New Orleans and set about getting her affairs in order. She was not sure when Slade would return, but she hoped it would be before she left. It did not take long for her to sell the shop; the building was prime real estate in the French Quarter.

On Friday morning she picked up the money from the real estate agent on Chartres Street. From there she proceeded directly to the cathedral and put five hundred dollars in the poor box. She said a prayer of thanks to Madame Le Fort for her blessing and prayed for guidance for herself and Slade.

When she came out of the cathedral, Slade was waiting for her. She threw her arms around his neck and wondered what life would be like once they were far apart. She could see he was thinking the same thing.

Slade carried a big, gift-wrapped box. He had signed a record contract, and the company had paid him a ten-thousand-dollar bonus, but he had to be back in New York at the beginning of the week. New Orleans was about to be history, so they went to Galatoire's for a farewell lunch.

Friday afternoon at Galatoire's was a tradition in New Orleans for those who could afford it on a regular basis. It was also a tradition for those who could not afford it but went anyway.

"I never did tell you the story of how I was able to pay for that first lunch," Slade told Isabella. "There was an obnoxious tourist from Columbia, South Carolina, in the bar the night before. He was drunk as a skunk and heckled me for hours to play 'Dixie.' I wanted to cut his tongue out. 'We don't know that goddamn song,' I finally screamed at him. The man pulled a hundred dollar bill out of his wallet and tore it into three pieces. He put one piece in front of each of us.

" 'Learn it!' he hollered."

" 'Key of C,' I called out, and the band played on."

But this time lunch was different. They were rich, at least for the day, and they were going to order like they were rich.

Mahogany blades on polished-brass ceiling fans turned as slowly as the pace of life itself in New Orleans. Mirrored walls gave an instant view of the entire restaurant from any table. Caesar, a waiter there, was one of Slade's most loyal followers. He saw them when they entered and steered them to his section. Seated in the far back, they could see the entire drama of Friday at Galatoire's.

"Ceasar, we'll be here for a while. This is a celebration." Slade beamed.

"Take as long as you like, my friend. That's why I'm here."

"We'd like a bottle of Cristal and a pitcher of fresh orange juice to start."

They drank mimosas and ordered an array of appetizers: shrimp remoulade, crawfish salad, pommes de terre soufflé, and gumbo with piping hot baguettes and lots of butter.

A local TV newsman named Teddy, another regular at the bistro, came over and sat down at the table. He was celebrating his freshly pierced ear and showed off his new earring—a dangling silver stem of okra. Slade told him about his record contract and Isabella's sale of the shop, and Teddy immediately ordered another bottle of champagne. A little while later Slade called all their friends and invited them to lunch. The wild, motley group arrived en masse—to the amusement of some patrons and the disgust of others. Today they were gypsies in the palace, and more food poured out of the kitchen: pompano en papillote, crab meat omelettes, speckled trout meunière, and more champagne.

The party grew to a sizable mob, and tables were moved and added until they stretched half the length of the room. Teddy stood on a chair at the end of the long table and tapped an empty Cristal bottle with his knife.

"I have a little bon voyage present for Isabella and Slade." He cleared his throat and sang a beautiful a cappella rendition of "Do You Know What It Means to Miss New Orleans." The guests hugged each other and wept and drank more champagne.

Slade stood at the other end of the table and picked up the big box. "I usually prefer to let my fingers do the talking, but this is a time for words of thanks." He lifted his champagne glass. Tears streamed down his face, and he turned to Isabella. ''To Isabella Rivière, my lover and my friend. May the wind always be at your back, and may your horizons always be blue.''

Isabella rose from her seat and clinked his glass with hers. They drank and tossed their glasses over their shoulders and embraced in a long and tender kiss to roaring applause.

''What's in the box?'' Teddy called out, and Slade remembered the present. He set the box down in front of Isabella.

''Something you may need again.''

Isabella opened the box and lifted out the old ship's clock she had brought from the *Basil M. Gelder*. It had been polished and repaired, and it shone brilliantly.

She lifted the clock out of the box and placed it on the table, just as the bells began to chime at the stroke of midnight. She poured another glass of champagne.

''To Slade Patterson,'' she said, ''the man who taught me that love could be more fun than work, that music is the voice of the soul, and that lunch should last forever.'' She drank her champagne and tossed the glass directly at the clock. The brand new crystal cracked neatly in two, and the bells were silenced as the hands of the clock froze on twelve.

The next morning, Isabella and Slade boarded the train for New York. They sat in the last two seats of the club car, facing the rear so they could look back at the land where they had shared so much.

''Friends for life,'' Slade said, pouring the last of another bottle of champagne into their glasses.

''Amis pour la vie,'' Isabella echoed.

The sun disappeared behind a pearl gray cloud and

turned the sky to silver. A flock of hungry gulls followed the train across the Rigoletes Bridge at the entrance to Lake Pontchartrain, and from the rear platform Isabella tossed small pieces of bread into the air for the birds. All the while, Slade played Hoagy Carmichael's "Star Dust" on the old piano in the bar car—to the delight of their fellow travelers.

Paris

It had been raining in Paris for several days. The rain anchored most people to sidewalk cafés, where they spent long afternoons sipping combinations of coffee and liqueurs to keep them warm and take their minds where their bodies could not go.

Isabella cheerfully greeted Philippe, her waiter, and Christophine, her chef, when they came in to begin preparations for what her faithful clientele called the best lunch in Paris. Déjeuner toute la journée was the specialty at Chez Bar-B-Q Hill. A few years back, when she had found Christophine, Isabella retired from preparing the whole menu, but she still made the desserts daily—and today was strawberry shortcake day.

She put a Slade Patterson record on the stereo and sipped her lait chaud, a mixture of milk and coffee. It was the taste of her youth on the island of Martinique. She listened to the colorful melodies and thought back on all the adventures that had brought her to this small café with the strange name on a tiny street in the heart of Paris.

Soon the sun came out, and the wet street began to give off steam. Isabella strolled down Rue du Dragon toward St.-Germain-des-Près, waving to her neighbors as she walked. The rain had washed the air clean, and patches of blue sky appeared overhead; people began popping out of doorways like rabbits coming out of their holes.

It seemed as if she had walked on cobblestones most of her life, from Saint-Pierre to the unrestored streets of the French Quarter to the tiny streets of the Sixième Arrondissement, but this lovely little break in the weather reminded her of a time and place where she never wore shoes and the streets were sand.

Isabella laughed to herself, took off her shoes, and continued to the Rue de Buci, following the fragrance of the marketplace, where she always shopped for the ingredients to make her desserts.

Today was indeed a strawberry day, and she planned to bake tiny sweet cakes with a hint of coconut and banana. She would cover them with mounds of fraises and crème chantilly.

She walked on, barefoot, into the marketplace, and, Paris being Paris, she drew not even a glance from the passersby wearing fashionable chaussures and chaussettes.

With a huge bag of strawberries in her arms and her shoes hung around her neck, Isabella walked back through the narrow streets to her restaurant. Philippe saw her coming and opened the door. Just as she stepped inside, it began to rain again.

The room was already full, and Isabella glided from table to table, saying hello to everyone on her way to the kitchen, leaving a trail of strawberry fragrance as she went.

She piled the fruit in the sink and began to wash it

as Christophine moved efficiently through the kitchen preparing lunches and singing.

The menu at Chez Bar-B-Q Hill was a lifeline of Isabella's travels: crab farci, pumpkin soup, big river shrimp from Martinique called oussou, and her famous coconut wedding cake. From her days in New Orleans she concocted gumbo, shrimp étouffée, crabmeat omelette, and a brisket recipe from Tujague's. From her days on Snake Bite Key she cooked up West Indies crab salad, oyster-and-bacon casserole, sweet potato pecan pie, and strawberry shortcake.

Each dish was a wonderful memory, and each day as she ate her lunch, she relived times, people, and places.

When she had finished washing the berries, Philippe seated her at her special table, where a steaming dish of red beans and rice and hot sausage was already waiting. She leaned over the bowl and inhaled. She closed her eyes, and when she opened them, she looked up, as she always did. For in front of her, above the door to her restaurant, was the parting gift from her first lover long, long ago. He was right: She had needed it more on land than on sea. The crystal was cracked, and the hands both pointed stoically to the number twelve.

Isabella gazed around the warm, friendly restaurant and began eating her lunch. She thought about Slade Patterson and smiled as she recalled the day when she had stopped time.

Margaritian Madness

YOU CAN'T TAKE IT WITH YOU

Lance Larimoore III is the only remittance man I have ever met. Before income tax was invented and life wasn't so complicated, a flock of black sheep from wealthy families was in constant movement around the globe. To the relief of their prim and proper families back home, they were beyond the borders of embarrassment, for they could always pick up their remittance far away, at their next port of call.

Lance, it was said, came from railroad money. He had married, joined the marines, fathered six children, lived in Greenwich Village in the heyday of hippiness, and eventually wound up in Margaritaville. He was sent a check every month, provided he never came within a hundred miles of his family again.

Lance lived the good life in old Margaritaville. It is told that on several occasions he took all the patrons of Tony's Tattoo Parlor on a ferry ride to Havana where they vacationed at Lance's expense until they drifted back to Margaritaville across the Gulf Stream.

Lance was eventually cut off by his family when they hired a new law firm. He received a form letter one day from Dewey, Cheatem & Howe, informing him that his final remittance was forthcoming. Lance Larimoore III reluctantly entered the job market.

He was no fisherman, and religion was surely not his calling. He also was not willing to live in a thatched hut on the wild, untamed part of the island. So he found himself in the other main line of work in Margaritaville—behind a bar.

I first met Lance at the outside bar of the Island Hotel, the local watering hole also featuring great food. This was back in the days before dress codes, three-hundred-dollar-a-night hotel rooms, and tourist development commissions, when pirates were still welcome on the island.

Lance had been thrown out of just about every bar in Key West at one point or another and was now the day bartender on the deck overlooking the Atlantic Ocean. Everyone knew you could find anybody you needed to talk to there. So a lot of people just chose to do what little bit of business they had under the sprawling poinciana tree. Frank and Lola, the owners of the hotel, were like parents to him and always gave him his share of second chances.

I lived right next to the kitchen exhaust fan. It directed torrents of greasy air through my apartment so that my bedroom, living room, and bathroom constantly reeked of onion rings. I had spoken to Frank and Lola several times about raising the vent, but things move slowly in the land of soon-come, and I finally had to take action to get their attention.

I put a Slim Whitman record on my turntable so it would play endlessly, cranked up the volume, pointed my new JBL speakers at the restaurant, locked my apartment, and left town for the weekend. When I returned, the vent had been fixed.

I had come back and was celebrating by spending a lot of time at the bar in pursuit of a beautiful woman in a slinky pink dress I had spotted there.

I woke up one morning on my porch swing when Lance bicycled past on his way to work. He was singing an old Joan Baez song and laughed aloud between verses. I stumbled next door to the bar to find out why Lance was so unusually festive and charming at this hour.

"It's a great day to be alive, Jimmy," he said. He was busy with his preparations behind the bar. "Especially since I woke up this morning set on committing suicide."

"What stopped you?" I asked.

"You got a minute?" He was mixing his juices.

"I got all day."

"Well, it won't take that long." He opened a beer and slid it down the mahogany counter toward me. Radar, my cat, climbed down the branches of the poinciana tree and lit on the end of the bar. She stretched the way humans wish they could, and then she sat as if waiting to be served. Lance poured her a champagne glass of half-and-half and began his story.

"Well, I decided I wanted to kill myself the moment I woke up. I'd thought about it a couple of times before, when I was hung over. The world I'd created for myself just never quite fit together; it was like a jigsaw puzzle with a couple of big pieces missing. But I would always lose interest because planning your departure from this life is no easy task. The labor of living always got in the way, but this morning was different because I had a method—a glamorous, foolproof method.''

The phone rang, and I thought Lance was reaching to answer it, but instead he pulled the cord out of the wall and hurled the phone into the sea. ''Goddamn phone company,'' he muttered.

He came back to where Radar and I were seated. He poured a little more cream in her champagne glass and opened another beer for me.

''I thought I would walk into the ocean and drown myself in the Gulf Stream waters, just like Hart Crane did. I walked out onto my porch and stared at a passing ship and thought about poor, misunderstood Hart Crane, floating for those few seconds in the tropical air between the lights of the ocean liner above and the phosphorescent wake of eternity below. I would join him soon.

''I found a piece of rope on an old lobster trap that had washed up on the beach, and I made myself a hangman's noose—I knew how to do it from my Boy Scout days. Then I swiped a cinder block from the construction site next door. That was one of the reasons I was killing myself—because even Margaritaville is turning into a first-class tourist trap, and the condo commandos are moving in next door.

''Anyway, I cradled the heavy block like a baby and walked into the water. The sun had just come up, but it was already hot, and that block started to get real heavy, but I was determined to reach deep water. I walked about a mile, but the water only came up to my knees, and that fucking brick wasn't getting any lighter."

Lance tramped up and down behind the bar, pantomiming his attempted voyage to the bottom of the sea. I was laughing because I knew that a huge mud flat ran south for about two miles in front of Lance's house, and the water was never more than waist-deep.

"That's when I heard the phone ring in my house. I turned and looked back to the shore. It seemed like a million miles away. And then I remembered I hadn't left a suicide note, so I started back. Whoever was calling would be my last link to the cruel world, and they could alert the media. My friends would be sad, my family would be glad, but in the tropics, they come and they go.

"I stumbled out of the water, hoping I wouldn't have a heart attack before I could kill myself. When I got to the porch, I loosened the noose and freed myself from the cinder block. I lunged through the front door to grab the phone.

" 'Don't hang up,' I screamed at the mystery caller. 'This is Lance Larimoore III, and I'm going to kill myself! You're the last person on earth I'll be speaking to, and I want you to tell the world that it won't have Lance Larimoore III to kick around anymore!' "

Lance fell to the floor behind the bar and rolled into a ball, clutching his stomach. I stopped laughing and ran behind the bar to see if he was okay.

"Are you all right?" I yelled. He pushed me away with his hands and nodded.

He finally caught his breath. "It was the fucking phone company calling to tell me they were shutting off my phone for not paying my bill! The goddamn telephone company saved my life. Besides, it was a long, long way back out to the Gulf Stream, so I decided to come to work today."

I ran into Lance on Salt Street yesterday. He had just been fired for the two hundred and fifty thousandth time and needed to borrow fifty bucks. He told me he was working in the laundry room at the Creola Hotel folding bed linens. The big Cuban woman who ran the laundry had accused him of making up his own working hours.

"Were you?" I asked.

"Well, yes," he answered bluntly.

I gave him the fifty dollars and watched him trot on down the street to the Island Bar, and I was glad the phone company had spared Lance Larimoore III from the longest walk of his life.

ARE YOU READY FOR FREDDY?

Local news reporters, minicams, and cops had gathered in front of the Seashell Searcharama. A strong scent of hair spray was in the air as the truck driver spiffed up before giving an eyewitness account of the accident.

According to him, the big tractor trailer filled with rattlesnakes and alligators had been bound for the Faron Fang Serpentarium, and he had slammed on the brakes to avoid twelve huge bales of marijuana that had fallen out of the sky from a dope plane being chased across the treetops of the Everglades by a DEA helicopter.

The trailer jacknifed across the highway, blocking traffic in both directions.

God, I love South Florida. Another typical day. I put my Falcon Sprint convertible in gear and made an end run through the big tomato field on the left side of the highway. The army of police was too busy chasing snakes and confining people to their cars to notice me.

I dodged two big rattlers who looked like they could

puncture my tires. Then I bounced on through rows of little green tomatoes and drove up onto the old Card Sound Road.

Card Sound Road is the back door to the Florida Keys, a straight line going south. It is a two-lane blacktop lined on each side by a stand of Norfolk pines, a road on which speed limits are meant to be broken. It ends as abruptly as it begins, leading back to U.S.1 near Key Largo, the territory of Travis McGee and Humphrey Bogart. I was going all the way to the end in Key West where I would catch the ferryboat to Margaritaville and celebrate my return from Nashville.

When I passed the first hand-painted sign that read "Blue Crabs for Sale," I knew I was close to Alabama Jack's. It was an old watering hole with some kind of magic attached to it. I could always find a little peace of mind there, sitting at one of the wooden picnic tables overlooking the water. I had definitely reached a crossroad.

After years of being flat broke, I was carrying a cashier's check for fifteen thousand dollars in my pocket—my advance from the record company. I could go home, pay all my bills, and plunge head on into trying to make a career out of music, knowing the number of people who made it to the big time could fit on a pinhead. Or I could take the money and invest in a shrimper heading south to do a little "square grouper" fishing and triple my money in a month. It seemed to be either crime or punishment, and either way I'd be up to my ass in alligators. I needed to have a beer and just sit and think.

I was *not* ready to see a silver, pink, and black rock 'n' roll tour bus smack-dab in front of Alabama Jack's.

It was parked under a cypress tree, like a chariot from another planet. Painted along the entire length of the bus was a large mural that would have given Salvador Dali nightmares. I knew instantly that the commander of this spacecraft was none other than Freddy Fishstick, the lead singer of Freddy and the Fishsticks! My favorite rock 'n' roll band!

Freddy and the Fishsticks had come out of Hattiesburg, Mississippi, and wound up in California where they made the big time and were the hottest act on Parrothead Records. They were a legend to aspiring musicians all over the South. Though their popularity had peaked a long time ago, they still toured on the "dinosaur" circuit, playing their vintage hits for diehard fans like me.

I walked through the door of Alabama Jack's and saw Snake Larson, the drummer, and Boomer Boggs, the bass player, shooting pool. Cleaver Johnson, the guitar player, was hunched over the Wurlitzer between two young blondes in bikinis who were helping him pick songs. A couple of old crabbers sat at the bar smoking Camels and nursing their beers.

I got a menu and walked out to the porch. From my seat at one of the picnic tables, I watched a small sailboat moving down the serene canal toward the bridge. I wondered if Freddy was still asleep in the bus. I had never met him, but I had just come back from cutting a record in Nashville—in the same studio where he'd made so many classic albums. It had been a dream come true.

Suddenly a big tarpon flew out of the water and into the air—about ten feet from my table. I stood hypnotized as the fish hung up there for what seemed like an hour and then landed on its side, splattering water all over the porch. My T-shirt was soaked.

"Jesus H. Christ!" someone shouted. "What kind of fish is *that*?"

"Tarpon!" I yelled at the phantom fisherman. "If you want him to stay on, bow toward him with your rod when he jumps."

"How the fuck do you bow to a fish?" he yelled back. I was on my feet, running to the far end of the porch. The fish jumped again. He shook his head vigorously from side to side, rattling his gill plates. This dislodged the hook, which sailed through the air—right at me. I instinctively raised my hand to cover my face, and the hook sunk into my forearm.

"Shit!" the fisherman and I hollered together.

Fortunately the barb was still visible. I gave a quick jerk.

"I think this belongs to you," I said, and when I looked up, I realized I had been hooked by Freddy Fishstick.

"Jesus, I'm sorry, man. Are you okay? You're bleedin'. We got a first-aid kit on the bus. I was just tryin' to catch a couple of snappers, you know. Come on."

I followed him to the big bus parked under the cypress tree. The door swung open, releasing a cool rush of air.

"Push Rod, grab the first-aid kit. I done hooked me a human." The big bus driver lifted himself out of the driver's seat and hurried down the aisle to the back of the bus.

"Just call me Freddy," the singer said. We shook hands, and he looked me straight in the eye. "Wait a minute. I know you. You're that new kid on the label. I been hearin' about you. Buffett, right?"

"Jimmy."

"Well, I hope you don't think this is how I get people into my band. You say that was a tarpon, huh?"

"A big tarpon. What were you using for bait?"

"A live shrimp about as big as my finger. When that big bastard hit, I was just thinkin' about nothin' and lookin' down into the water. Where I come from, the water is brown."

Push Rod came back with the first-aid kit, and I poured a little peroxide into the hole in my arm and put a Band-Aid on it.

"Where're you off to?" Freddy wanted to know.

"To Key West, and then to Margaritaville."

"Key West. That's where me and the boys are goin' to."

They had just finished a gig at Tobacco Road in Miami and had a few days off. Freddy had never been to Key West, but an old friend was going to meet him there.

The other Fishsticks came shuffling back to the bus, and Freddy introduced me to everybody—except for the young blond girls who had come along, and they introduced themselves since the band members couldn't remember their names.

"Well, Jimmy, the least I can do is buy you lunch—that is, if I could catch a ride with you the rest of the way." He looked over at my convertible parked in front of Alabama Jack's. "I been cooped up in this bus for a long time, and it's too pretty a day to stay inside. Feels like a rag-top day to me."

He grinned at Push Rod. "I'll meet you at the hotel in Key West."

Push Rod just nodded, sucked on his toothpick, and

fired up the big diesel. The bus moved slowly out of the parking lot, climbed to the summit of the Card Sound Bridge, and disappeared into the mangroves.

"Let's eat," Freddy said.

We went back to the porch and sat at the magic table where the big fish had introduced us, and I told Freddy my problem. He listened while I described how the shrimpers in Key West wanted me to captain the boat, and he just sat there with a stern look on his face.

When I quit talking, he nodded and finished chewing the hushpuppy in his mouth. He washed it down with a swig of beer.

"I've made twenty-two albums, had eight go platinum, won two Grammys, and I've played around the world for nearly twenty years. I think I could be of some help, and since you say this here's your spot for deep thought, I guess I was just meant to come along and tell you what I know."

It's not every day that a hero pops into your life and goes from a photo on an album cover to someone you're sharing your tartar sauce and your life with. The voice of experience was sitting across the table, and I was going to listen to what he said.

"How did you get into show business?" I asked.

Freddy wiped his mouth with a napkin and laughed. "I got into music to meet girls. I was raised a good Catholic boy in Biloxi, Mississippi, and when I went off to college, I couldn't wait to make up for lost time. I went to school in Hattiesburg, and my roommate was this crazy guy from Alabama named Teddy Paris, and he played the guitar.

"Well, hell, the women at the fraternity parties would just flock around him and goo and gaa. So I asked him one day if it was hard to play the guitar. He said anybody could do it. He only knew three chords, but they'd brung him more girls than any man in Mississippi. So I got him to teach me those chords. It was easy enough. I started playin' beer joints all over the South. Spent a good number of days on a stage with just a piece of chicken wire between me and death from flyin' beer bottles.

"I remember the first job I ever had. I was playin' in a trio in a folk club, and it was one of those days where I was just bustin' strings right and left. We finished the first set, and the owner, the son of some Mafia type, was more interested in humping waitresses in the coat closet than in what transpired on the stage. He made the first and only musical critique I ever heard from him: 'You break too many strings. If you break any more this set, you're fired. Loosen them up.'

"I tried to explain that the tension on the strings was what sort of made the goddamn guitar work, but by then he was talkin' to the waitresses again. Hell, my first job was on the line, and I asked my partners what they thought I should do. 'Loosen the sonsofabitches.'

"I unwound my strings and just beat the hell out of the front of the guitar for forty-five minutes and told jokes I'd heard at the shipyard where I was workin' in the day, and I didn't break another string. At the end of the night, I was sittin' in a chair wipin' the blood from around the sound hole of my guitar, and the owner came up to me and said, 'See, it worked.' Lesson One: Never forget—they are always the enemy."

Freddy paid for lunch, and we took off for Key Largo. I told him about the old bar where they'd filmed the movie *Key Largo*, with Humphrey Bogart, and he definitely wanted to stop there. We got back onto U.S.1, and he did his imitation of Edward G. Robinson talking about the pompano dinner.

"Your bus is great. What's it like being on the road?" I asked.

"We call the bus the Sub 'cause it's a whole other world. I live half my life in that bus, and my band is family. The intimacy of an eight-by-forty-foot aluminum box on wheels teaches you a lot of patience, and you start learnin' that the best guitar player in the world ain't worth it if he's an asshole.

"I had this one guitar player back in another band who was always bitchin' about everything—the food, the gigs, the girls, his salary, the record company. One night I reached my bullshit tolerance level and told him that if life on the road was so goddamn intolerable, he could tell it to the Gila monsters. I dropped him off in the middle of the fuckin' desert in Arizona. He caught up with us at the truck stop the next mornin' and apologized, and he stayed until the end of the tour, but that's when I went and found Cleaver. Cleaver not only can play with the best of 'em, but he's also a great guy. Lesson Two: Just remember, assholes are born that way, and they usually don't change."

"I remember seeing you on the cover of *Rolling Stone* when you and the lead singer from Cats In Heat got married on that train tour up in Canada," I said. Freddy rolled his head back and looked up at the blue sky.

"Desdamona." He laughed. "Now that woman was from another planet, but I was as much in love with her as anybody. She died and moved to the suburbs, but we still keep in touch. I got married a couple more times, but they never lasted. It took me a while to figure out I was more married to my lifestyle than I could be to any one woman."

We pulled over at a little bait and tackle shop, and I helped him pick out some jigs and plugs for his spinning rig. He wanted to stop somewhere to fish if we had the time. My urgency to get home to Margaritaville was evaporating.

"That train tour was about as crazy as it ever got. I don't think I slept from one end of Canada to the other. Cats In Heat was the opening act, and I remember runnin' into these crazy fuckers up in British Columbia who were pot farmers. They loaded us up with a bale of sensimilla, and we stayed high all the way across Canada till Carla, that was Desdamona's sister, gave a bag of pot to a Mountie in Montreal, and we all got arrested. Lesson Three: You do not want to go to jail.

"I spent my honeymoon in jail, and we were divorced by the end of the tour. Those were naïve days. Hell, we didn't know dope would kill us back then. If I'd known I was gonna live this long, I would've taken better care of myself."

We pulled into the parking lot of the Caribbean Club. Inside, pictures of stars of *Key Largo* hung on the walls. A couple of bikers from North Carolina recognized Freddy and asked for his autograph. He signed napkins and then insisted that they get my autograph, too, though they'd never heard of me.

"This kid's going to be famous one day. You wait and see." Freddy started laughing. "Fuck trucks," he said. "Hearin' about North Carolina reminded me of where it happened."

"What?" I asked.

Freddy sat down at a small table under Lauren Bacall's photo, and the bikers came over with a pitcher of beer.

"It was one of those crazy nights after a show. We'd played the Naval Academy in Annapolis, and we were running to Knoxville. Hicks, my lighting director, had been hit on the head by a big power cable that fell out of the riggin' the night before, and he got himself a slight concussion. He was a little out there, anyway. Snake and I stayed up all night talking to Push Rod. It started to snow somewhere in Virginia, and the roads were terrible, and we weren't making good time, but we sure as hell were having one.

"Hicks was sipping steady on a bottle of Chivas Regal. He said it helped his concussion. He had a big white bandage wrapped around his head—real funny because it accentuated his bald spot. Well, he finally passed out on the couch, and Snake and I got a couple of colored markers out and decided we were goin' to make Hicks a new man. We drew circles around his eyes and put a big ol' Frankenstein scar on his cheek, and finally we wrote 'Fuck Trucks' in big red letters on his bald spot. We went to bed around sunrise and left Hicks on the couch with his makeup job.

"Push Rod stopped for coffee at a truck stop and forgot about our artwork so Hicks didn't know. The poor sucker got out to go eat breakfast. I guess he went to take a leak and saw himself in the mirror, 'cause he shot out of that place and hid in his bunk till we got to Knoxville.

"That was one hell of a day. And to top it off, another bizarre thing happened. We were all up in the front of the bus listenin' to the radio when we pulled into town, and we heard news reports that I'd been killed in a plane crash in Virginia. This was pretty alarming, and I stopped right away and called my folks to tell 'em the reports of my death were highly exaggerated. That night when we opened the show, I just put my tour jacket on a mike stand and played offstage. The people didn't know what to think, and when I walked out at the end of the song, you would've thought I *had* risen from the dead."

The bikers whooped and toasted to Freddy's rebirth, and one of them said he'd been at that concert in Tennessee and remembered it as if it were yesterday. Elvis came on the jukebox singing "Suspicious Minds," and Freddy was off again. He sang along with Elvis in his Elvis voice, and most of the people who had come into the bar gathered 'round, and before we knew it, we had a party. The song ended to clapping and hollering. Freddy sat back down.

"I got to tell you about the invasion of the Elvis imitators," he said. "I was asleep in the back of the bus, and Push Rod pulled into some hotel on the outskirts of Philadelphia where we were staying. He would always leave the generator runnin' and the air conditioner on, so I could sleep on the bus 'cause it was usually a lot quieter than the hotel lobby early in the morning. Well, when I got up around noon this particular day I was sort of in a fog, and I walked up to the front of the bus to pick up the key to my room. Push Rod always left it on the dashboard. I saw this guy standing near the bus. He was wearing a white Elvis outfit with the rhinestone cape, and people were takin' his picture.

"I walked out, and he looked at me and went into a

karate pose, and I just kept walkin' to the lobby. But then I saw another one. This guy was in all black and was talking to another Elvis who was black in an all-white suit. I thought, 'This is it, Freddy. The road has finally gotten to you.' I went into the lobby, and there were three more Elvises—in a gyrating contest. I ran to the elevator and went straight to Push Rod's room.

" 'I don't know what a nervous breakdown is supposed to feel like, but I think I'm having one. Everyone in the world is startin' to look like Elvis Presley!' I shrieked. Push Rod just started laughing.

" 'This isn't funny,' I said.

" 'Yes it is. They're having an Elvis-imitator convention here.' "

Well, the bikers from North Carolina and the tourists from New Jersey went wild. They said that in *their* book, Freddy—not Elvis—was the king.

We walked out to the old dock behind the bar where Humphrey Bogart had let that rotten Johnny Rocco have it through the hatch on the boat. We left the memories of Bogey and Bacall behind and headed on down the highway. We didn't feel the heat of the day until we were stopped by a long line of traffic just east of Marathon.

"Goddamn drawbridge is stuck!" someone yelled from one of the cars in front of us.

"This happens a lot down here," I told Freddy. "Last time the bridge got stuck, the only guy around who could fix it had a wreck on the way here, and they threw him in jail for drunk driving. So the bridge stayed up for a whole day."

Freddy got out of the car with his spinning rod, pulled a new plug lure out of his tackle bag, and joined the other bridge fishermen on the catwalk. He heaved the lure a long way out toward the power poles and brought it back with a jerky motion. On the third cast he hooked up, and a few minutes later he hauled a big snook out of the clear water.

I carefully unhooked the fish and tossed it back into the water. It lay on the surface, stunned for about half a minute, and then it slashed its tail from side to side and dove for the shelter of the bottom.

''When I retire, I'm goin' to do this all day,'' he said and tossed the line back out.

''It must be nice to think about retiring. Hell, I'm just thinking about getting started.''

''Don't worry. I've been threatenin' to retire every year lately. Then I think about what else I'd do, and I know that playing music is it. Guess I'm just meant to bop till I drop.

''The closest I ever really came to throwing in the towel was up in Missoula, Montana, ten years ago. We'd been on the road for about eighty-five days, starting in Boston. By the time we got to Montana, all of us were right on the edge. Boomer had snaked Snake's girlfriend, and they'd gotten into a little scrap at the hotel bar before the show. I didn't know about it.

''Well, we arrived at the concert site—a rodeo arena. The wind was blowing so hard that the whole stage was covered in red dirt, and to beat it all, someone on the student activities council had decided they'd try to break the Guinness world record for kegs of beer consumed in a three-hour period. I walked onto the stage in the windstorm and looked out at ten thousand pitchers sloshin' a sea of beer under the big Montana sky. What the hell, I thought, I'd seen worse-lookin' crowds back on the bar circuit, and this was the big time. I waited for the usual vamp intro and offstage introduction and took my cue and stepped out to play.

"I hit the first chord of my guitar, but there was no drum downbeat or bass guitar entrance. I looked around at my band and saw Snake and Boomer rollin' around on the stage beatin' the crap out of each other. The audience loved it. They thought it was part of the show. The rest of the band was stunned, and the promoter was already skippin' out with the Haliburton briefcase full of cash.

"From where I was standin', I sort of knew how Custer must have felt when he saw the Indians sneakin' up through the prairie grass just a hundred miles or so away. I was going to die on stage. I would be beaten to death by a drunken, angry mob of college students armed with Tupperware pitchers, and my poor mama would have to read about it in the paper. All this was goin' through one side of my brain, while the other side was singin' the opening song.

"When I got to the bridge, I walked back to the fight and kicked Boomer in the ass and caught Snake on the side of the head with my Stratocaster. I raised my clenched fists over my head and screamed, 'Rock 'n' roll!' The crowd went crazy. I spun around in a flash and glared at Boomer and Snake. I hollered that this was *my* stage, and they could fight on their own time, but while they were up here, they'd play music, or I'd crack their skulls open on the spot.

"I guess I scared the shit out of 'em, 'cause they picked up their instruments and played the rest of the set. That night on the bus, I sat in the front seat next to Push Rod with a .357 Magnum strapped to my side and dared anybody to say a word. I got off the bus at a friend's house in Livingston and went fishing. I'd *had* it. I didn't need that kind of shit.

"A couple of days later, after I spent mindless hours walkin' the banks of the Yellowstone River castin' for trout, I rejoined the band in Memphis. Snake and Boomer had cooled down, and by the end of the tour the Battle of Blood Valley State College was just another hilarious memory. That's the way it goes. We're just high-paid clowns in the first place. Lesson Four: When you start to take this job seriously, you're in trouble."

A wave of cheers spread rapidly down the line of cars from the crippled bridge in the distance, and the bridge began to fall back to earth. Freddy reeled in his line, signed a few autographs, and jumped back in the convertible.

"Just another magic day in show business," he sighed.

"I hope you don't mind me asking you all these questions," I said, "but I've never met a big star before, and I'm just tryin' to figure out a few things for myself and get some hints from somebody who's been there."

"Jimmy, I'm a wealth of useless information, but you're welcome to all you want. Only thing is, if you want to keep asking me questions, you're gonna have to buy me somethin' to eat. This sea air has my appetite up."

I had driven down the Overseas Highway many times, and I always noticed the distances between the keys got longer as you headed farther out into the ocean where the railroad once ran to the end of the sea.

We crossed the Bahia Honda Bridge, and this provided us with a fantastic view of what gave these islands their signature. Green and turquoise water swirled around the white sand flats and formed natural murals that stretched to the horizon. I pointed out the small puffs of mud near the bridge and told Freddy they were made by a large school of bonefish feeding on the incoming tide.

We descended back to sea level and rounded the curve onto the east end of Big Pine Key. I pulled the Falcon Sprint into the parking lot in front of the Big Pine Inn. The cool, dark, pine-paneled foyer was a welcome relief from the heat outside, but there wasn't a soul in sight.

We heard signs of life and followed the voices to the bar. A tall, thin bartender was chatting with a table of patrons who drank and played cards in air-conditioned comfort. The black waitress told us they didn't serve dinner for another hour, but her husband had just brought in a fresh batch of stone crabs. They would be ready in fifteen minutes if that would do. We assured her it would.

"Are you from Barbados?" Freddy asked.

"How'd you know?" She smiled the kind of smile that made me think she'd rather be in Barbados than at the Big Pine Inn.

"Your accent. I spent some time down there a while back, doing some recording at Lagoon Studios. Land of rum and flying-fish sandwiches."

She kindly showed us to a table in the old dining room. A white grand piano sat in the corner, a relic of better days. The Big Pine Inn predated the railroad and had been built by Mrs. Gussie Zeigner. She had all the pine and cypress shipped in by boat and erected the finest inn of its kind in the Florida Keys at that time. During the twenties, the Big Pine Inn had been a gambling hall and nightclub. When prohibition came along and the Point became a hot spot for contraband from Cuba, the inn saw its share of dollars changing hands between rum runners and bootleggers.

"Is there any place you haven't been?" I asked.

"Africa. I always wanted to go to Africa," he said in a dreamy voice.

The waitress returned shortly with a pitcher of beer and a platter piled high with crab claws. We attacked with hammers, tiny forks, and mustard sauce.

"You a singer or somethin'?" the waitress asked.

"Some people think so. I spent a whole month in Barbados and loved every minute of it."

" 'Tis a beautiful island. One day I'll get back home."

"God, recording in the islands! That must have been a trip," I said and reached for another crab leg.

"It was a fuckin' nightmare at the time. Now it's funny. The people on the island were great, but the manager of the studio was the most tight-assed Limey on earth. He couldn't *stand* us havin' so much fun. He charged us by the drink at dinner, so I bought the bar. He didn't allow local people up at the studio, so we hired a wild Rasta band from the bush to do backgrounds. But the thing that really did him in was hidin' the women from us."

"What do you mean?"

"Well, we worked for a whole month, real hard, and we'd go hang out at this little bar down in Bridgetown after work. We'd usually wind up jamming with the local band, and then a limbo contest would start, and the party went on into the next mornin'. We hadn't seen any women other than locals for a long time, and then one night I walked into the bar, and there was a table full of beautiful English girls. I was immediately set on findin' out who they were, and the bartender told me they worked at the studio.

"I had never *once* seen them at the studio, so I went over to the table and introduced myself. They laughed and said they knew who we were, but the studio manager had told them to stay away from the crazy Americans or they'd get fired. That was all I needed to hear.

"Well, we had a party that night, and I made sure it would be the talk of the island—especially the naked orgy in the swimming pool when we shot Roman candles at the studio manager's cottage and sort of set his roof on fire. I led the naked bucket brigade, and we saved his house from burnin' to the ground, but I don't think he was very appreciative.

"He never talked to me after that, and it was fine with me. That is, until he got roaring drunk one night and decided to cuss me out. I let him get about halfway through his character assassination of me, my country, and American musicians, and then I hit him. The whole bar applauded.

"He passed out in a boat that night, and somehow it came untied, and he drifted out to sea. By the end of the day, they'd found him, but he was looking pretty bad. Lesson Five: It takes no more time to see the good side of life than it takes to see the bad.

"When the album came out, I thanked all the wonderful people on the island, the mystery women who worked at the studio, the dogs, the cats, and the taxi drivers. At the very end of the list was the studio manager's name. He'd put himself at the end because of his attitude.''

We finished off our second lunch of the day with Key-lime pie, said good-bye to our Barbados waitress, and started on the homestretch.

It wasn't long before I turned onto Eisenhower Drive and realized I'd come halfway around the Gulf of Mexico. Fatigue had started to take over. But then Freddy cracked a joke, and my energy came back, at least for a few minutes. Freddy was watching a disturbance on the public boat ramp where a boat trailer, boat, and truck had slid down into the water, and a fight was breaking out on the dock.

''That's just the weekend crowd at their best,'' I told him. ''Spend the day out on the water in the hot sun drinking beer, and you can't remember the brake pedal from the accelerator. I used to work there.''

''Doesn't look too interesting to me,'' Freddy yawned.

I had been a one-man audience for a one-man show for the seven hours it had taken us to get to Key West, and it had pretty much helped me make my big career decision. His stories made me want to have my own, so that in a decade or so, I might pass on a few pieces of advice to some young kid looking for answers. I almost passed the Sub. It was parked beside the El Rancho Motel. I put on the brakes.

''No, I'm not staying there. If you don't mind, you could drop me off wherever you're goin', and I'll call my friend.''

I drove to the ferry dock to catch the last boat to Margaritaville, but saw that it was empty. Captain Popps ambled out of the engine room companionway, covered with grease.

"When you headin' home?" I asked.

He spit a mouthful of tobacco juice to the side and said, "Not tonight. Goddamn propeller just spun right off the shaft near Jellyfish Key. Mel and the boys found it on the bottom with the magnetometer and are bringing it in now. Frank and Lola and a bunch of your partners in crime are all holed up at the Midget waiting for you."

"Any excuse for a party," I said.

Captain Popps sniffed at the air. "Yeah, I can feel a gravity storm comin' on. Be careful, you know what can happen to you in this wildass town."

I went over to the southernmost phone booth and called my friend Lydia. She sounded very happy to hear my voice and invited me over.

Freddy was standing in front of the shell vendor's stand where Willie, the conch-salad man, was doing his rap to a group of tourists. Behind him a big, faded Stop sign stood with its back to the Atlantic Ocean—indicating we had run out of highway.

"This is the end of the road, Freddy," I said.

"Not for me, Jim." He walked over to the seawall and stood staring across the water for a moment. The wind blew his long hair, and the sun illuminated the lines around his eyes.

"I've never played in Havana, but I always wanted to. Who knows? Fidel may be a fan. The longer I stay around, the more I realize anything's possible."

"Why don't I just drop you off at your friend's house?" I asked. "The ferry isn't going out, so I'm not in any hurry."

Freddy got back in the car and read me the directions to his friend's house. I drove slowly down Atlantic Avenue looking for the street address when I heard a familiar voice call out a foreign name. "Frederick Purvis, where the fuck have you been?"

"Brother-in-law!" Freddy answered.

Lance Larimoore III was crouched behind a hibiscus bush. I had not seen him since the first day he had moved back to Key West and had gotten into the exterminating business. "Barflies to real flies," he had told me weeks ago at the ferry dock. He had on a weathered safari hat and was taking aim at a fly on the wall with his red, fly-killing gun. He pulled the trigger, and a flat, white projectile shot out across the porch and pinned the doomed fly against the wall.

Lance looked down and inspected the dead insect at close range. He reloaded his gun and said, "Vincent Price was in town last week. I just wanted to make sure it wasn't him. Enough hunting for today." He took off his pith helmet and came over. Freddy met him halfway.

"I didn't know you two knew each other," Lance said.

"We didn't. We hooked up at Alabama Jack's this morning," Freddy said. I looked at my Band-Aid and laughed.

"I didn't know *you* two knew each other," I said.

"You never asked. Frederick and I go way back. He was married to my sister in a former life."

"Desdamona?" I asked.

"You hit it," Freddy said.

"Can I get you a beer?" Lance asked.

"No, I'm going to Lydia's house. I'll see you later."

"Well, we'll be out there," Lance said. I walked back to the convertible with Freddy, and he picked up his fishing gear.

"Thanks for the ride," he said.

"The pleasure was mine."

''Hang in there, kid. Just remember: Don't ever listen to 'em.''

''Who?''

''All the people who'll tell you how you have to change your life in order to be really successful. Most of them've never been there, so don't listen to 'em. It's your choice. You've got to want it more than anything in the world, and when you get it, the trick is to figure out how to keep it from killin' you or going crazy. Lesson Six: If you decide to run with the ball, just count on fumbling and gettin' the shit knocked out of you a lot, but never forget how much fun it is just to be able to run with the ball.''

''Maybe I'll catch up with you somewhere out on the road,'' I said.

''Jimmy, you can pretty much count on it. Hell, there are only two hundred people in the world. Don't you know that?''

''No, I didn't know that,'' I said, ''but I'm beginning to learn.''

MAY 3, 1989

I was so exhausted that night fifteen years ago that I never made it out of Lydia's house. I woke up the next morning and found myself the only passenger on the boat to Margaritaville. Captain Popps had fixed his prop. There had been some party in Key West, alright, for when my friends finally got home, they told me how Freddy and the Fishsticks had taken over the Shipwreck Lounge and had rocked the joint until dawn, then piled onto the bus with a bunch of vacationing airline stewardesses and headed for their next gig in Tampa.

Last year I was in Sydney, Australia, winding up a tour of the Pacific. I was doing some last-minute shopping for friends and family back home and took a cab out to Paddington where you can find one of the great marketplaces of the world on Saturdays. I bought clothes from Bali, Aboriginal posters, eucalyptus oil, and tea-tree cream, and I spent the last of my Australian money before taking off for Los Angeles that evening. I walked back to King's Cross, and as I strolled past a stretch of record shops, Thai restaurants, and hippie clothing stores, I saw a handbill pasted on a store window:

This Weekend Only
Freddy and the Fishsticks
Monkey's Uncle Bar
Paddington & Ross
8 PM – Midnight
No Cover, No Minimum

I found the address of the club and went inside. I was almost overcome by that essence of bar-funk bouquet—pine cleaner, stale beer, and cigarette smoke. An old Filipino was sweeping up, and I asked about the band.

"Fleddeee be gone to Blisbane. He no here no more. Back next weekend," he mumbled. I left a note for Freddy with the old man and left for the airport.

That night, as I settled into my seat for the fourteen-hour ride from Sydney to Los Angeles, I pulled out that card I had written up so long ago—the world according to Freddy. I reviewed the lessons one by one.

Lesson One: Never forget—they are always the enemy.

Lesson Two: Just remember, assholes are born that way, and they usually don't change.
Lesson Three: You do not want to go to jail.
Lesson Four: When you start to take this job seriously, you're in trouble.
Lesson Five: It takes no more time to see the good side of life than it takes to see the bad.
Lesson Six: If you decide to run with the ball, just count on fumbling and getting the shit knocked out of you a lot, but never forget how much fun it is just to be able to run with the ball.

The rules hadn't changed much. I thought about my old friend asleep in a bunk somewhere on an unfamiliar highway. I ordered a brandy and looked out the window of the 747 and raised a glass to Freddy and the Fishsticks.

"Bop till you drop," I whispered, knowing it was as much for me as it was for him.

Son of a Son of a Sailor

HOOKED IN THE HEART

To this day *The Old Man and the Sea* is one of my favorite books. I have read it at least a dozen times, and the characters are like close friends. You don't see them for long stretches of time, but when they suddenly appear again, it is as if they never left.

I still have my first copy of the book. Someone gave it to me for a Christmas or birthday present long ago, and it has traveled well because it is small. I first read it when I was eight years old. The relationship between the old man and the boy is what was most touching, because it reminded me so much of my grandfather and me.

Yesterday I had a pretty good day out bonefishing, exercising the "gray ghosts of the flats." There is an energy in these waters like nowhere else; the headwaters of the Gulf Stream squeeze between the land masses of Florida and Cuba, and the collision and overlapping of the Gulf of Mexico and the Caribbean Sea affects human and animal behavior in more ways than Heinz has sauces.

When I hung my fly rods back in their racks on the ceiling, I accidentally knocked a book from the shelf. The familiar faded blue book lay on the floor.

Instead of returning it to its place on the shelf, I mixed myself a rum drink, settled down in the Florida room, and opened the book to the first page.

A flock of roseate spoonbills landed gently in the salt pond across the canal to find their supper in the shallow water, and I worked my way comfortably into the couch with *The Old Man and the Sea*. I read the first chapter and the description of the old man in the village, and I looked at the photograph on the wall above me. It was a picture of Jane and me, taken with Gregorio Fuentes, the real-life "old man."

Several years ago I hooked up with a documentary film crew retracing Hemingway's hangouts with the help of his son and granddaughter. I threw in with them for a chance to go to Cuba.

When the Hollywood circus comes to town, I am always amazed to see how the chance to be on camera—or just make breakfast for the cast—completely transforms people. They will lie, cheat, steal, quit their jobs, commit acts of adultery, fall in love for the weekend, and sell their children into slavery just to say they are in the movies.

I was as much a victim of this plague as anyone. And when I was contacted about composing some music for the project, I agreed to forgo my usual fee for the chance to accompany this ship of fools aboard the old schooner *Western Union* on her ninety-mile crossing from Key West to Havana.

The whole time I had lived in Key West, Havana had intrigued me, especially the tales of the "old days" when the ferryboats made daily runs to the casinos and art deco hotels. Life here was much more connected to Cuba than to America.

Before that, my grandfather's sailing ships constantly called on Havana, and I had read many of his old logbook and journal entries. This added to my vision of the city. It had been the hub of activity when the Spanish first entered this hemisphere. My father had spent his first birthday on board a ship in Havana harbor, and when my grandfather raised all of his signal flags into the rigging to celebrate, so did every other sailing ship in the harbor.

We left Key West at midnight on the old schooner, sailing under a crescent moon. We arrived off the Cuban shore around noon the next day and were greeted by a pair of patrol boats manned by young boys shouldering AK-47s. Our stony faced escorts took us past the skyline of Havana and then into port.

We were driven by car down a boulevard that stretched for miles. It was lined with large, unoccupied houses. When we finally reached the city, we were taken to the Hotel Habana Libre. We checked in and found a microphone dangling from an air vent in the bathroom. I quickly composed a song entitled "Speak into the Shower Stall, Please" and sang it into the little condenser mike, wondering who was listening on the other end.

I wasn't due to work until that night, so Jane and I set out to look around and take in the sights, all two of them. The entire afternoon we were followed by secret police who seem to have watched too much "Yankee

TV,'' to judge by the way they popped in and out of doorways and hid behind signs, tailing us to the Floridita restaurant. I waved and yelled for them to join us for lunch, but they quickly buried their faces in their newspapers and tried to look nonchalant.

We ordered daiquiris and stone crabs that came from the deep waters near the old Morro Castle. Then a trio sang ''Guantanamera'' in perfect harmony while we drank a bottle of Rumania's finest wine.

After lunch we took in the Museum of the Revolution, which is sort of like a little commie Disney World. The boat Fidel came ashore on sits in a bubble, and an old airplane hangs from a wire above. Cisco and Pancho were still hot on our trail. We meandered through Old Havana past the ancient cathedral, and I was reminded of some sections of Paris—except for the hundreds of vintage Chevys, Fords, Pontiacs, and DeSotos parked on the cobblestone streets.

That night I was to perform for the film in La Bodeguita del Medio, which was, in its day, one of the great bars of the world. In prerevolutionary days, Fidel, Salvador Allende, and Papa Hemingway were regulars. There they discussed the fate of the world over *mojitos*, a wonderful rum drink for which the bar was known. Now La Bodeguita del Medio attracts Canadian tourists and Russian workers on holiday.

The film crew was busy at work, and the place was packed with stony faced ''customers'' checking out the film crew at work. I finally spotted Cisco and Pancho in the corner and sent them a couple of drinks, but then it was lights, camera, and action time. There I was, singing ''Havana Daydreamin' '' to a bar full of cops who did not have a clue about who I was, what I was doing in Cuba, or what I was singing about. Nevertheless, they were wildly enthusiastic when I finished the song and bought us lots of *mojitos*. I love show business.

We stayed until closing time, but our Foreign Ministry guides left early, so we took a cab back to the hotel with Cisco and Pancho following us in a black '53 Ford. Driving through the dark, deserted streets of Old Havana, I felt as if I were in an old "Boston Blackie" episode.

Our cab driver was checking us out in the rearview mirror, and I'm sure it wasn't hard for him to figure out we weren't working for the government. He switched the tape from a Cuban salsa band to the Rolling Stones, double-shifted the car, and took the turn onto the main drag with his tires squealing. He flashed an excited smile at us, raised a clenched fist, and shouted, "Rock 'n' roll."

The next morning Peter, the producer of the film, called me much too early and asked if I wanted to go out with him to meet Gregorio Fuentes. He said he was waiting to get permission from the Foreign Ministry to go out early.

I had heard this old man was the inspiration for one of my favorite books, and I was not going to miss the opportunity to meet the man behind the myth. We gathered in the lobby and waited for the Foreign Ministry people to show. But after almost two hours, we took off without them. This gave Cisco and Pancho a morning workout they were not expecting.

We lost them at a downtown intersection when we changed taxis and soon were out of the busy city and on our way to Cojímar, where Gregorio lived.

The cab dropped us off at the entrance to the village, and it was like stepping into the first chapter of the book. We walked down sand streets past the old battery that guarded the harbor, and in the center of town we came upon a monument that had been erected to Hemingway.

Cojímar was still a fishing village. No tourist information booths, no beach rental stands, and this day we were the only gringos in town. It was very hot, and no breeze blew in from the ocean. We stopped for a couple of beers and got directions to the old man's place. We found him sitting on the porch of a small stucco house behind a bougainvillea hedge, smoking a cigar almost as big as he was. From the road, we introduced ourselves, and he motioned for us to join him on the veranda.

Peter was our interpreter and told the old man what we were doing there. The old man just seemed happy to have visitors and immediately launched into a fishing story, telling us of a fish he had caught last week. It had cut his hand badly. He raised his right hand and pointed to the fresh, deep cut, but it could barely be seen among the hundreds of other scar lines—an occupational hazard.

Although I could not understand Gregorio's words, I felt what he was communicating. The story of his life was in his eyes and his hands. He wanted to show us his new boat in the boatyard on the east end of the beach, so we walked over together, followed by young inquisitive faces that darted in and out of our path like hungry minnows. I asked the old man if Papa Hemingway had left him any mementos, thinking he might have a classic rod or reel or cherished photos. He took a long draw on the cigar, looked up at the sun, and patted his heart with his hand.

Walking beside him down the beach, I asked if he had ever seen the movie version of *The Old Man and the Sea*. He had, but he didn't seem too flattered by Spencer Tracy's portrayal. When we got to the far end, Gregorio showed us his boat. It was a small skiff painted the color of the sea, and his eyes lit up as he told us of encounters with marlin so big they dined on sailfish. He showed us the marks on the bow of the tiny boat where sharks had attacked, and again he looked at his hands and pointed to a scar—the mark of yet another adventure.

We sat in the shade of a mahogany tree, and he told us a story about the time they were making the movie version of the book. The original director was fired and replaced by someone from the studio in Hollywood. Gregorio and Papa were fishing in Argentina when Hemingway heard the news. He went on a rampage and told Gregorio they were going back to Cuba to shoot the new director.

They boarded the plane in Buenos Aires for Havana, Hemingway wearing two pistols and carrying a bottle of rum, which they finished quickly. Apparently news of their impending arrival and proposed intentions were enough to cause the studio's director to lose interest in the film, and by the time Gregorio and Papa were back in town, the original director was rehired and on the job. Gregorio said Papa looked around, and, finding everything to his satisfaction, they were on the next plane back to Buenos Aires and fishing for trout the following day.

A large party was waiting to greet us when we returned to the old man's house. Cisco and Pancho were across the street in sweat-drenched suits, and our escorts from the Foreign Ministry very politely informed us that we were not to go anywhere without them in the future. We made our apologies, and then the old man said something to the young bureaucrats. They looked like children who had just been given a good scolding.

The film crew began to unload, and Cojímar buzzed with the preparations for the next day's shoot. I was so glad we had been able to share that little piece of time with the old man. He seemed absolutely content with his life as a fisherman.

God had given him the talent to bring to the surface fish larger even than the boat he used to pursue them. He didn't reject the fame and notoriety, but they were just secondary—spin-offs of his true talent. He was a model for growing old gracefully. His boat was his country, and he was the undisputed king. The political Cuisinart whirring away on dry land was of no concern to him.

The *Western Union* rounded the fort and entered the harbor with all her sails flying. We walked down to the pier where she would be docking. The town came alive with the arrival of the ship, and it was like being in another time. We boarded the boat, and Gregorio puffed away on his cigar, his eyes glued to the women in the crew; they scurried around the deck in bikinis. He looked over to the town square at a big crowd of excited teenage boys rattling on in Spanish, and he started to laugh. Peter asked what was happening, and Gregorio pointed to the women on deck and then to the boys on shore. "All those young boys are wondering why I am down here with all the pretty girls."

I noticed Cisco and Pancho perched up in a gumbo-limbo tree with their binoculars trained down on us, and I waved.

We were skimming the waves in my seaplane on our way out of Cuba, and flying fish as big as the plane leaped out of the water and swam in formation with us. I had jet engines now and was moving amazingly fast when I saw a small boat at twelve o'clock.

I descended gently into the ocean, and there was Gregorio, sitting in his little blue skiff, holding a hand-line and eating a mango. He invited me aboard for breakfast.

Suddenly one of the giant flying fish grabbed the line and started pulling the boat. We were off on a Nantucket sleigh ride. I panicked. My airplane was drifting away, and I was about to jump out of Gregorio's boat when he warned me that huge sharks surrounded us. I would be eaten alive. He pointed to the giant teeth embedded in the transom of his boat.

Next I knew, the fish was pulling us past Sand Key Light, and I saw Key West in the distance. A pink Coast Guard plane circled overhead. I said my good-byes to Gregorio and swam for the distant shore.

The airplane noise now sounded more like a mosquito in my ear, and I slapped at it and woke myself up. There was a little smear of blood and mangled wings; I had scored a direct hit. My copy of *The Old Man and the Sea* lay open across my chest, and crickets in the night-blooming jasmine began their symphony.

I walked outside with the dream still in my head and stared up at the clear sky, marveling at the fact that I lived on a little plug of dirt in the middle of two great oceans. I thought about Gregorio and wondered if he might be staring at the same stars from the other side of the Gulf Stream.

LIFE IN THE FOOD CHAIN

I took a friend of mine for a leisurely sunset sail through Key West harbor on a cloudless Sunday evening aboard my little mahogany sloop, the *Savannah Jane*. She has served my sailing needs for nearly ten years now and will certainly suffice until the next strain of "big boat fever" infects me.

A ten-knot breeze was blowing from the southeast when we slipped the lines and sailed away from the dock. The wind is pure necessity on board the *Savannah Jane*—she has no engine. A solar panel powers my running lights, stereo system, and VHF radio. A few years ago I made some modifications down below and installed an oversized icebox; this is more important to me than an engine.

That day, for the brief little excursion, I brought along a slab of smoked amberjack, a container of conch salad, a baguette of French bread, a jar of Grey Poupon mustard, a roasted chicken, fresh salsa, chips, a box of

Carr's crackers, a couple of KitKat bars, Evian water, a bottle of Santa Margarita Pinot Grigio, and the ever-present emergency ration of peanut butter and jelly.

It took longer to put away the stores than it did to hoist the sails and clear the point. My friend, who was not a sailor, watched me packing everything away and asked, "How long will we be out?"

"Oh, for about an hour."

"Why all that food?" he asked.

"Well, you may think it'll only be an hour, but when you go out on the ocean, you always have to anticipate the worst scenario and hope for the best."

I trimmed the mainsail and fell off the wind a little. This would steer us clear of the parade of boats returning up the channel from a day of fishing. We sailed for the cut between Christmas Tree and Tank islands. I tied off the rudder with the end of the main sheet and pulled out the bread and smoked fish and uncorked the bottle of wine.

I poured two glasses, and my friend offered a toast: "To another shitty day in paradise!"

After putting on Beethoven's Pastorale Symphony No. 6, I scanned the horizon, the wind gauge, and the knot log. At that moment I realized I was living my life about as well as I could. The sun was preparing a colorful departure to the other side of the world, and the breeze was holding steady. I offered my friend another glass of wine and steered west toward Archer Key Basin.

We slipped in silently and came upon a school of happy tarpon feeding along the flats toward the mangrove island to the south. The fish swam through the clear water in time to the music. I opened the container of conch salad and spooned tasty bits of conch, hot pepper, and lime juice onto a cracker. Overhead, an osprey dove for the shallow water, plucked out a small fish, and climbed back up to altitude.

"What if the wind stops blowing? What do we do then?" my friend asked.

"Eat the chicken and wait for the wind to blow. But if the tide is against us, and we get out into the stream, we could wind up in the Bahamas or North Carolina."

He stopped chewing and looked at me. "Are you serious?"

"Serious as a heart attack." His questions triggered memories of the unpleasant day that led to my current recipe for sailing.

Part of the folklore of my family is the story of an incident that occurred when they all made a voyage with my grandfather aboard the sailing ship *Chickamulla*. I grew up hearing the tale told from many points of view, and then one day, it came back to haunt me.

"Let me tell you a little tale about life in the food chain," I told my friend.

It all started when we were cruising about five hundred feet above Nantucket Sound in a chartered Aztec plane, and it was a perfectly beautiful day. Below us, the water was covered with little triangular sails, and I couldn't wait to pick up my boat in Nantucket and join the weekend armada.

My friend Semmes was with me, but Semmes is not what you would call a "man of the sea." He had been jaded by his last voyage, a trip from Ft. Lauderdale to Key West in a howling norther. He spent a terrifying night lashed to the wheel to keep from being washed overboard. The boat he was sailing on had a near-miss with an oil tanker near Sombrero Light.

"I looked up and all I could see was this giant 'U' coming out of the night," Semmes said. "Then I realized it was the second letter of the word *Gulf*, the first word of the name of a ship, the *Gulf Empress*. The giant 'U' was welded to the bow of a tanker about to slice us in two. I had been seasick most of the night but was cured instantly by raw, naked fear. We *narrowly* escaped the oncoming ship."

I showed Semmes the proximity of the two islands we would be sailing between, and I promised to buy him dinner as soon as we got to the Vineyard.

After the plane landed we had a bowl of chowder and a couple of beers at the Opera House. I grabbed two more beers, and we took off for the old North Wharf where the *Savannah Jane* was tied up.

We passed the A & P, and Semmes said, "Maybe we should stop and pick up some Triscuits and 'squirt' cheese."

"Oh, that would just spoil your lobster dinner."

The *Savannah Jane* was in her slip, ready to go. We were soon on our way into the harbor and made good time down the channel. The wind was blowing steady from the southeast, and the knot log indicated seven knots. If it held, we would be home on Martha's Vineyard in under three hours. I measure time at sea by tapes, and this day looked to be a three-tape sail.

I put on the first hour—a collection of my favorite sailing songs—and trimmed the main as we rounded about for the Vineyard at the last channel marker. Semmes took the tiller, and he relaxed a little. I was happy to be able to demonstrate that there was a better way to sail than what he had last seen. Joni Mitchell sang about the Greek Islands and, in the distance, Martha's Vineyard began to take shape; the topography of the land came into view. By now, Semmes was singing along with the Beatles. I felt the wind drop slightly and trimmed the sails.

Then, just off the eastern tip of Tuckernuck Island, the knot log displayed a digital "goose egg" as Jimmy Cliff wailed through the still air about "Sitting in Limbo." The boom began to pitch back and forth as the slack big mainsail responded to the motion of the sea. The *Savannah Jane* was becalmed.

Semmes looked at his watch and saw that dinner hour was near. "Enough of this Long John Silver shit, Bubba. Let's crank up the engine and get on in before it gets dark."

"I don't have one," I said.

"One what?"

"One engine." I turned off the tape player to save the battery for the radio. His stomach growled, and he stood up, only to bang his head on the boom. We had stopped yachting and had started surviving.

We were still becalmed when the sun went down, and the outgoing tide pushed us south into shoaly water where no other boats ventured—especially at night. I managed to raise the marine operator on the radio and got a message through to my house that we wouldn't be home for dinner. We would dine aboard the yacht instead.

Semmes squeezed himself down into the tiny cabin and rummaged through the storage bins, hoping to find something to eat. He cursed, not finding anything. The two beers we had brought on board were long gone. He grunted and groaned, and then the first positive sounds came from below.

"Find something?" I shouted. He thrust his long arm out of the companionway. It was holding a small can of evaporated milk. He uncoiled the rest of his body and inched his way to the cockpit.

"You look like you've seen a ghost," he said.

"I may have."

"What do you mean?"

I took the rusted can of evaporated milk and held it in my hand.

"When my father was a child, he was becalmed at sea once, off the coast of North Carolina. My grandfather was the captain of an old sailing ship, the one I mentioned named the *Chickamulla*, and he had brought his family along on the voyage from the Turks and Caicos islands to New York.

"The wind didn't blow for twenty-eight days, and they ran out of food and water and were near starvation when my father, who was eight years old, found a can of evaporated milk rolling around in the galley. He pried it open immediately and was gulping it down when the old black cook came upon him and hustled him up to my grandfather for punishment.

"My grandfather looked at my father and the precious milk dribbling down his chin. 'I cannot punish my child,' he said. 'My son was hungry. What was he going to do but eat?'

"A few days later they were finally spotted by a passing ship and given supplies. The wind came up, and they sailed on to New York. Their story made the front page of the old *New York Herald*.

"My grandmother never made another trip on a boat.

The old *Chickamulla* stayed in the family until she was towed to Mobile Bay and abandoned in a small bayou beside Highway 90. While I was growing up, I saw it every time I crossed the bay."

By the time I finished telling Semmes my story, the fog had thickened, and the distant foghorn signaled its whereabouts punctually. I opened the can of milk and poured about three-quarters of it into two cups and put the tin back in the cooler.

"That's breakfast."

We clinked our plastic cups, and Semmes said, "To the ghost of the *Chickamulla* and Captain Buffett. Thanks for dinner."

I finished my milk and checked the anchor light to make sure it was illuminated and tried to sleep. Semmes went below and repositioned himself around the mast step and was soon snoring. He seemed to be taking this rather well, all things considered. The wind indicator showed a little breeze was picking up; we would probably be home for breakfast.

The first light of morning barely filtered through the dense blanket of fog, and the little breeze had died or moved off. I could not see the bow of the boat, a mere fifteen feet away.

"This stuff is as thick as pea soup."

"Don't mention food!" Semmes called out from below.

The absence of airplane-engine noise overhead on what should normally be a busy weekend in the skies led me to believe the whole Cape was socked in. The marine forecast on the radio confirmed it.

Semmes and I drank the last little bit of milk, but this time without toasts or frivolity. Our moods were darker than the gray fog surrounding us. I finally contacted a friend on the Vineyard and gave him what I thought was our location. He told me he would get to us as soon as the fog lifted. Around noon, I got a call back; they were under way and should be at our position by two o'clock.

The wind never did pick up, and twenty-four hours after we had left Nantucket for a leisurely three-hour sail, we were being towed to port in Martha's Vineyard. Our rescuers had brought a pack of bologna, a loaf of white bread, and a jar of yellow mustard. It tasted like filet mignon.

Semmes ate seven sandwiches before we reached Vineyard Haven, and, with a little nourishment in his system, his vivacious personality came back to life. He and the captain struck up a long conversation about a mutual friend in Colorado.

We slipped the tow just outside Lambert's Cove, and I turned the music back on. Cat Stevens chanted about longer boats, and we sailed in on the rising tide. A breeze had returned and blown the fog up to Nova Scotia, and it was, again, a picture-perfect day. I was not interested in the scenery, though. All I wanted was a hot shower, a plate of hot food, and a warm bed. But Semmes had told the captain of the towboat we would stop by his store in Edgartown for a drink.

I politely went along and minded my manners. We crawled through thick ferry traffic and eventually found the place. I was totally on autopilot and stumbled through the front door, oblivious to my surroundings.

The captain showed us his collection of artifacts: old coins, cannonballs, and rusty bits and pieces of armor and weapons. He had salvaged this flotsam from various wrecks in the area. I wasn't paying much attention to his talk, though. I found myself, instead, drawn to the big oak table in the middle of the room.

In the center of the table, a large book lay open. A two-page photo of a sailing ship was spread before me.

"Semmes! Come here!" I called out. He came over and looked at the photograph.

"Too weird," he said. We both stared down at a photo of the *Chickamulla* at anchor. And that's the end of the tale.

The sun lowered itself into the sea. I poured the last of the wine, and we toasted the simple but elegant departure of the big round ball. Then the wind stopped.

"Oh no," my friend said. "What's going on?"

I whistled softly, calling for the wind to return—like an old man in Antigua had taught me to do—and surprisingly the breeze returned. My friend breathed a sigh of relief. He shoveled a heavy portion of salsa onto his chip and asked, "Whatever happened to Semmes?"

"He retired from sailing. He went back to making pizza in the mountains, and I brought this boat south to Key West."

We rounded the beacon at the harbor entrance, and I gauged my distance and let go of the main, gathering it in. The boat glided down the narrow passage between the boat slips, and we lightly touched the dock at our mooring in front of the Waterfront Market.

A GIFT FOR THE BUCCANEER

The Yucatán Peninsula, another one of those mysterious names that conjures up visions of the tropics, stretches like a thumb trying to close a circle around the Gulf of Mexico by touching the index finger of Florida. However it doesn't quite make it. This leaves about four hundred miles of open water through which the Gulf Stream escapes on its journey to Ireland.

I had been on the road longer than I wanted to be, especially since the tour took place in the hard-core months of winter, and we had been facing an endless onslaught of cold fronts, one behind the other, from the frozen North all the way across the Midwest. The last show was in Chicago in late February, and, as always, I decided to treat myself to something good for surviving yet another tour. After all, living well *is* the best revenge.

En route to the last show we were trying to find O'Hare Airport in a snowstorm, and I heard myself singing the words of an apropos song I had written years ago in similar conditions: "I gotta go where it's warm." We began our descent, and after tightening my seat belt, I studied the world temperature section of the *Sun Times* in one hand and the *Official Airline Guide* in the other. Florida was cold, and it was raining in St. Barts, but the Yucatán Peninsula was basking in sunshine.

I had never been to the land of the Olmec and the Maya, but I had always been intrigued by what I had read about the ancient civilizations that had flourished along the swampy seashore of the southern Gulf of Mexico. The airline guide listed a nonstop flight from Chicago to Cancun the morning following our last show, so I called Jane and arranged for her and our six-year-old daughter, Savannah, to meet me in Cancun. Our travel agent in Miami booked us into what she described as a "simply fabulous waterfront villa," and I played the show that night in snowy Chicago knowing that early in the morning I would be on my way back to the tropics.

Possessing a vivid imagination can make the bitter pill of reality a lot easier to swallow, but it can also cause the pill to get stuck in your throat. My vision of where I was going was based on two movies. First, I remembered the Tampico street scene in the opening frames of John Huston's *Treasure of the Sierra Madre* when a prepubescent Robert Blake badgered Humphrey Bogart into buying the winning lottery ticket. Second, I thought of the not-so-hot resort hotel in Tennessee Williams's *Night of the Iguana*, where beautiful expatriate American women rocked slow and lazy in cotton hammocks on a veranda that overlooked the sea. They were clad in halter tops and muslin skirts and drank enough to lose their religious guilt but not their style. Unfortunately, Cancun turned out to be a place where life did not imitate art.

The ride from the airport was your obligatory twenty-five-mile cab ride that seems to be standard in Third World tourist countries. Personally, I would rather pay the same rate and have them build the damn airport next to town and avoid the long ride. But I'm used to bad roads and bad drivers from my years of living in the Caribbean, so I started the slide to island time by drinking a beer and stretching out in the back seat, promising myself that I would start to learn a little Spanish when I got home.

The hot, dusty ride on the Mexican mortar field known as Highway 307 wasn't as bothersome as what I saw through the broken window of the cab. High-rise buildings lined the beach as far as the eye could see. I wondered if the Maya had invented time-shares and left them with us as a curse on the land. My vision of Ava Gardner walking down a deserted moonlit beach to skinny-dip evaporated instantly. No, she would not be here—for I had landed in a tourist trap.

The driver deposited me at the entrance of Casa d'Oro, where I would find my fabulous oceanfront villa. The ride to town had prepared me for the worst, and it materialized in the shape of an off-yellow, long rectangular building, some kind of Holiday Inn in a former life.

I picked up my key from the bored desk clerk and made my way through a maze of laundry carts to find my room. I stared out the window, again looking for the waterfront. Immediate relocation was definitely necessary, and that would require the kind of inside help always found at the local bar.

Every tourist town has a place the people who work go to get away from the people they have to serve. I found the one in Cancun without much difficulty. I made myself comfortable at the Gringos bar and struck up a conversation with a bartender from Houston. He recognized me immediately (always a help in a strange land) and introduced me to Carlos, the manager.

Carlos bought me a margarita and thanked me for writing the song that had so helped his business, and I autographed a menu. Then Carlos and I had our picture taken together in front of the sea monster fountain. Making the best of a bad situation, my new best friend Carlos called his cousin at the newest luxury resort and found me a *real* beachfront villa. Another call to another cousin got me a rented Jeep, and Carlos handed me his new, portable, direct-dial phone, and I called Jane in the States to tell her what was going on.

One of my favorite songs of all times is "You Can't Always Get What You Want" by the Rolling Stones. There are a lot of bad songs, a fair number of good songs, and a few really great songs. A great song is more than just words and music. It's like a thumb pressing against the pulse of living that relates a simple truth about a very complicated process. I hummed the song and wiped the condensation from my giant picture window in my beachfront villa at the new hotel so I could finally view the water.

On the other side of the hermetically sealed glass, a gentle breeze swayed the palm trees, but I could not feel it: my picture window was bonded to the cinderblock walls. There were no sliding glass doors or small vent windows, and seeing my breath frost up in the overly air-conditioned room with no thermostat, I knew I was being protected from hurling myself to my death. Back in America those enormous hotels with the towering mass of rooms and Star Wars elevators opening onto a gigantic fern-bar lobby were prime locations for spectacular suicide leaps. But here in Cancun, the hotel management was safeguarding me from the three-foot plunge to the soft sand beach.

"But if you try some time, you just might find you get what you need."

No, you can't always get what you want, but I was a lot better off than I was a few hours earlier.

Jane and Savannah arrived early the next day along with an army of insurance salesmen from the Midwest who descended upon our hotel like a swarm of locusts. The sun was shining, and it was warm, so we ventured down to the crowded beach, set up our spot, sealed our ears with headphones, and each turned up our Sony Walkman to drown out the world. The Walkman is a wonderful little Japanese invention, but I am still not convinced that all the technical garbage they have sold us over the last few decades hasn't been programmed to detonate on December 7, 2000, bringing an end to the Western world that not even Jerry Falwell could imagine.

Jane picked up on a conversation taking place under a nearby beach umbrella—apparently the salesmen and their families were off to see the ruins at Tulum. We quickly scratched that one off the list of things to do, read through our Fodor's guide for alternatives to our present location (more and more resembling a gathering of beached white whales), and settled on a trip to a nearby little island called Isla Mujeres, "the island of the women." It was off the beaten path and promised a good meal, more serenity than we had seen so far, and the ruins of an old pirate mansion. The latter immediately sparked one's eternal, mysterious fascination with the rogues of the sea.

Way back when, on the shores of the northern Gulf of Mexico where I grew up, I had always been infatuated by the stories of Jean Laffite, the pirate king of Barataria. He was one of my early heroes, and my most precious possession at that age was a scale model of Laffite's flagship, the *Black Falcon*. My father had helped me build it. On the many trips we made to New Orleans in my youth, I always made my parents take me through Jackson Square past the statue of Old Hickory and his horse, and we explored the rooms of the Cabildo Museum, home to the artifacts of the rich past of Old New Orleans. The story of when Laffite and his crew joined forces with Jackson to fight the British was one of my favorites, and I brought it back to my playmates in Alabama. We endlessly reenacted the Battle of New Orleans in the E. R. Dickson schoolyard, and I always played Jean Laffite.

Jane, Savannah, and I crossed Bahia de Mujeres on a crowded little ferryboat from Puerto Suarez. The others on board included a few tourists, a lot of locals, and a herd of small goats. The breeze over the water felt good after the hot ride out in the rental car, and I read to Savannah about the ruins of the mansion. It was built by a notorious pirate named Fermin Mundaca as a gift to one of his future ex-wives. The woman, however, would have nothing to do with the old buccaneer, and she left "the island of the women" for greener pastures, leaving Fermin to build a tomb for himself near the mansion. Legend had it that the place was now haunted by the restless soul of the pirate, who had died of consumption in a bar in Mérida, leaving an unfilled grave as yet another monument to unrequited love. We thought of ruins comparable in scale to those of the Maya, the Citadel in Haiti, and the pyramids themselves, and we happily off-loaded our Jeep when we reached the ferry dock in the middle of town.

The white sand streets were deserted, for siesta time was in the air. One cheerful old woman was selling mango popsicles, so we bought three and asked for directions. She pointed us toward the paved road leading out of town.

We drove south, past the ruins that gave the island its name. Jane and Savannah scanned the horizon for signs of the pirate mansion, but as we rounded a bend in the road, they sighted a quaint little restaurant overlooking a pristine cove. The wind carried aromas of French cooking from the open-air kitchen, and our quest for adventure and discovery was temporarily put on hold; lunch in the present took priority over death in the past.

The restaurant, Kankin's, was run by a lovely woman originally from Normandy. She served us grilled lobsters and real *pommes frites* at a table overlooking Garrafon Bay. Over coffee, she assured us we were on the right road to the ruins. Our wanderlust had been tempered significantly by the food, and Jane and I were now more interested in a siesta than in the ruins, but we drove on.

I could not find the turnoff leading to the mansion, and I drove back and forth until Savannah spotted it.

We made our way down an overgrown path through hundreds of mangroves, creeping along in the underbrush, pushing back limbs and spider webs. Parrots flew from tree to tree overhead, and I had a little adrenaline rush when we finally spotted a clearing ahead, and I could make out a cul-de-sac in the distance. We had found the ruins.

Savannah and I jumped from the Jeep and set off to explore a dilapidated old building—surely the gatehouse to the great estate. Jane stayed behind to guard the Jeep and told us to report back to her as soon as we could.

We rummaged through the house and climbed mildew-covered stairs up to the second story, thinking of hidden treasure, cutlasses, and cannonballs. But all we found were piles of empty beer bottles and a rather large brassiere. I looked out through a big hole in the wall, hoping to see the grounds and the big house. All I saw were the tops of mangroves growing clear down to the Gulf.

"This is it," I told Savannah.

"This is *it*?" she asked.

"Well, the people were a lot smaller back then, and in those days this was a pretty good mansion."

"Whose is that?" she wanted to know, pointing to the bra.

"Maybe it belonged to the pirate princess," I answered vaguely. But she wasn't buying it.

Undaunted, she said, "Well, Dad, let's find the pirate grave."

Jungles are scary. We think we know about them from watching Tarzan movies and "Wild Kingdom," but there is a sense of awe and fear that remains locked in the human subconscious. It goes all the way back to the days of the cavemen, and it reminds us that we are truly out of our environment. Throw in the haunted grave of a bloodthirsty pirate, and you start to tread rather dangerously in the domain of the jaguar and the water moccasin. We eased our way through the underbrush, and, to my amazement, Savannah pointed to the tomb ahead.

We stopped, and I knew this was the time to be Brave Dad. We would march to the open door of the tomb and fearlessly confront the ghost of Fermin Mundaca, and, as Brave Dad, I would boldly inform the apparition that he didn't scare us one bit. But I was spared the confrontation with my own fears. For at that moment, a cry shattered the jungle stillness and every hair on my body stood at attention. I looked at Savannah, and all I saw was her mouth drop open. The pink bubble gum she had been chewing so violently dropped to the ground. She spun around and took off for the Jeep. I was right behind her.

Jane woke up as she saw us running, and we heard another cry in the distance. I leaped in and started up the Jeep. We sped down the drive toward the paved road.

"Was he home?" Jane asked tauntingly.

"I don't think so."

Savannah leaned between us from the rear seat of the Jeep, "Dad, what was that noise?"

"I think it was a jaguar or puma just letting us know we were in his backyard."

"Were you scared?" she wanted to know.

"Well, I didn't feel like he was exactly being friendly."

"No, but were you scared?" she persisted.

Enough of this cross examination, I thought. I am the adult here. I'll take the offensive. "Were you?" I asked.

"No," she said, matter-of-factly.

"Then how come that gum dropped right out of your mouth when you heard the noise?"

She looked at me calmly. "It was a gift for the buccaneer."

SOMETIMES I FEEL LIKE A RUDDERLESS CHILD

It was well into January, but the Christmas winds had not stopped blowing in. Gale warnings were still flying throughout the Lesser Antilles, and few sails were on the horizon. The low, steady roar of wind was just another routine sound as the island came alive.

On any normal day roosters crowed and the noise of a rock-crushing machine pulverizing a boulder were all a part of the Third World alarm clock on the island of St. Barts.

It was the morning after the night before, and I had only been asleep a few hours. Nestled comfortably under mosquito net, I woke when peacocks started fighting in the cashew orchard below my veranda. I opened one red eye. The ocean was covered with foam. African rollers crashed over the rocks on the eastern shore of Baie St. Jean, and the air was filled with a haze of salt spray. The rock-crushing machine had not yet started its attack. Then I realized it was Sunday, and slowly the fragments of Saturday night began coming together.

It had started as usual at Le Select, the bar in Gustavia, and had continued on at the Ranch, an all-night bar in the bush, where I had joined some other expatriate Americans who were playing bluegrass to the dismay of the disco crowd. The evening ended at Autour Du Rocher, a three-room hotel and bar I had bought part interest in, even after reading *Don't Stop the Carnival*. We had danced there until dawn. Somewhere in the night between petit punch and champagne, talk had come up about a sailing expedition to take Captain Groovy's boat to the British Virgin Islands for repair.

A big gust of wind roared through the house. It shook the roof and knocked a Haitian painting off the wall, sending my good luck gecko, Kaarem, scurrying up the wall into the attic. This was no day to be at sea. My guitar lay at the foot of my bed, and I carefully placed it into its case and climbed back under my mosquito net with a large bottle of Evian. In a few hours I would venture down to the Sodexa market and pick up a roasted chicken and a baguette for lunch. Later I would watch the video of *To Have and Have Not* and return to the sanctuary of my pineapple bed. There I would spend the rest of the day recuperating from what had been, to say the least, a B-I-G T-I-M-E.

I must have been asleep about fifteen minutes when I woke again, this time to the high-pitched sound of a straining engine climbing the hill to my house. I hoped the racket would stay in the distance, but I heard the car claw its way up the driveway. I did not have many visitors since I deliberately lived at the end of one of the worst roads on the island. It was notorious for puncturing tires and yanking tail pipes and fenders from the chassis. Whoever was climbing the hill to Maison Blanche this morning had to be on a mission.

The car came to a halt near my garage. I heard footsteps coming up the stairs and remembered something from the night before that sent me under my sheets to hide. I know who it was and why he was here.

"Oh, Bubba," a voice called out. "Mr. Son of a Son of a Sailor, the ocean is calling."

I folded myself deeper into the cool cotton sheets. "I am not responsible for anything I said after midnight," I called out.

"Come on, the sea air will do you good, and I have to get my boat to Tortola to get the steering fixed. Hell, with this wind, we'll be there in seven hours."

"It's blowing like stink out there, and besides, there is an old rule of thumb that my grandfather taught me: Never come out from under the mosquito net when the waves are over your bed." I peeked out from under my covers, and standing in the doorway of my bedroom was my good friend Groovy Gray, who had captained my boat when we first arrived in these waters on the *Euphoria II*.

"You promised you would help me take the boat to Tortola. I have to get the steering fixed before it goes out completely. I've got food and cold beer and the new Joni Mitchell tape."

"I like her old stuff."

Many years ago, Groovy and I had crossed a lot of ocean on *Euphoria II* listening to Joni. I had used my first record royalties to buy a boat. Tom Corcoran took my picture when the yacht broker handed me the keys, and that day I had been wearing a T-shirt with *Euphoria* written across the front. It was the name of a great bar I used to play at up in Portland, Oregon.

There was a look of contentment on my face like no one had ever seen before, and my boat was christened *Euphoria*. I paid cash for her, and she was my insurance policy. My line of work is not known for longevity, and if it was over soon, I could at least sail away to Tahiti on a beautiful boat and live happily ever after on a palm-lined beach in the Society Islands. She was rigged more for creature comforts than for speed.

I first met Captain Groovy in Key West when he was renting Sunfish to tourists at the Pier House, and I was the opening act for Coffee Butler and the Cups at Howie's Lounge on Duval Street. Groovy became a boat captain, and I became a rock star, and when I bought the boat, I called him and offered him a job; we went out looking for adventure.

Once we had steered the *Euphoria* through a narrow cut in San Salvador to escape a violent electrical storm. People lined both sides of the harbor entrance thinking they were about to see a shipwreck, but the gods were with us as we surfed down the front side of twenty-foot seas and shot the gap.

Another time we brought two old fishermen back from the dead, rescuing them and their demasted little fishing boat from a storm. We filled them with chocolate bars and coffee to get their blood pumping. Then we towed them back to the island of Anguilla and hopped a ride in a donkey cart while the dock people took them home. We made it to their town in time for their wake.

Fortunately, my music career proved not to be short-lived, but that meant I was spending less and less time on the boat. I sold her to some treasure divers who took her off to Lake Pontchartrain near New Orleans. Captain Groovy now had his own boat. It was a Swan 38 named *Zambido*, and he had sailed her across the Atlantic to St. Barts single-handed.

"Come on, Bubba. Joe's going, and he said to tell you that you were a weenie if you stayed in bed all day. We've all been in worse crap than this," he said. Groovy pointed out my door at the frothy ocean.

The right combination of guilt and machismo has sent many a fool out into the jungle when he should have stayed home. I climbed out of my bed, tossed a few clothes into my seabag, and was clipping down the hill before I knew it. I had a swim and ate lunch while Groovy went to get supplies. I set off for town and passed "Gasoline," who was walking toward the airport. He is an old St. Barts man who holds his nose and wears a bucket on his head so he doesn't have to smell the pollution that popularity has created.

I had seen Joe Giovinno the previous night in Le Select, and we had popped a bottle of champagne. A bee hung above the bar, and we hit it in the ass. Marius, the wonderful proprietor of the place, rang the bell, and we drank for free.

Later that night at the Ranch I saw Joe dancing on a table with several French girls. He had arrived a day earlier from Guadeloupe on his ketch, the *Viking*. I had seen him sailing into Gustavia as I rounded the hill below the statue of Jesus and stopped to watch him weave through the fleet. Years back we had met up in Provincetown when I first went north for the summer. After that we found ourselves on different boats in a lot of the same locations. He taught me how to sail, and I taught him how to sail with music. I always thought I got the better end of the bargain.

When our paths inevitably crossed, we used to sit around and tell each other sailing stories, and later they found their way into my songs. He was one of the best sailors I knew—one you trust with your life when the ocean is playing hardball.

"You have to feel the ocean," he used to say. "It is not something you are floating on. It is something that floats *in* you." He was not a Sunday racer, and he taught me that first and foremost the ocean is an unpredictable power.

Joe was sitting under the big shade tree at Le Select. I was walking across the street to join him when Groovy turned the corner; his Jeep was filled with supplies, and I motioned for him to come on over. He was in a hurry. Joe and I loaded the supplies into the dinghy and were soon on board the *Zambido*, anchored off the beach in Corossol, in front of the cemetery. He was leaving us no time to change our minds. Groovy was bouncing around on deck preparing to get under way.

"How in the hell did he get you out of bed today?" Joe asked.

"He said you were all ready to go and that you said I was a weenie if I didn't come," I told him.

"That's exactly what he told me *you* said."

"That sonofabitch," we said at the same time, just as the engine turned over.

"Can you guys give me a hand with the anchor?" Groovy yelled from the cockpit.

"We could swim for shore," I said.

"Oh, what the hell," Joe replied. "We're already here, and if we try and weasel out, he'll just get pissed off.'' He laughed a high-pitched laugh. ''We've been shanghaied.''

There were no other boats on the ocean that afternoon when we sailed out of Gustavia harbor. They all sat at anchor, and a few heads popped up out of companionways, wondering which crazy bastards were setting out to sea in this blow. We put a reef in the mainsail while we were still in the lee of the island behind Anse de Cays, and I saw the red roof of my little house on the distant hill above St. Jean.

Just for a second I closed my eyes as tight as I could and tried with all my might to transport myself back to my pineapple bed. I came out of my trance quickly when we sailed past the end of the island. The last Christmas winds snapped the mainsail tight, heaving the boat over, sending us crashing headfirst into the channel. Tortola lay seventy miles west across the Anegada Passage. Even on a clear day it could be one of the nastier pieces of ocean in the world.

''Pâté anyone?'' Groovy asked. He climbed up the ladder and held out a tray of hors d'oeuvres.

''You tricked us,'' I said.

''I didn't have much choice. I need to get this boat across, and I knew I was dealing with a couple of serious bed pigs.''

Thinking about other options only makes the real scenario worse. I learned a long time ago that you just have to roll with the punches, so we surrendered to our fate and settled in aboard the boat. I did not feel as bad as I thought I would, and I hated to admit it to Groovy, but I was actually enjoying being out at sea. The wind was blowing about thirty knots, and with the reefed main and a storm jib, we were still making a good eight knots. That would get us to Tortola by morning, and it would all be over. We would be on the dock at the Village Inn eating cheeseburgers and sipping frozen piña coladas. Things could be worse.

Joe said he was going to St. Thomas to see some friends after we delivered the boat. We ate the pâté and crackers and each had a cold beer. We tried to assemble the puzzle of the party the night before. Captain Groovy finally admitted he had felt just as bad as we had when he got up, but he had to fake a bunch of "health garbage" to shame us out of bed. I volunteered to stand the first watch and took the wheel. There was a good bit of play in it, but we would be on a broad reach the whole way, and that wouldn't require much steering. I watched the sun go down, put on a Michael Franks tape, and settled into my watch.

Joe relieved me shortly before midnight, and I went straight for my bunk. I hadn't been asleep long when I heard the cry for help.

I jumped out of the bunk, and Groovy was already ahead of me up the companionway stairs. There was no more rhythm to the movement of the boat, and I heard the halyards banging against the aluminum mast. It was raining hard, and lightning flashed all around. We were smack-dab in the middle of a bad-ass thunderstorm, and we were totally out of control. We had no steering at all and were striking the mainsail when a titanic wall of water seemed to just appear out of the dark night, and a huge rogue wave hit us broadside.

The main sheet tore loose from the jam cleat, and the boom whipped wildly across the deck. The reef points tore loose, and the big main had blown overboard. Joe and I were hauling it back on deck before it filled with water and became unmanageable. Meanwhile, Groovy was trying to secure the boom, but it got away from him.

"Watch out!" I heard him cry. I turned around, and the boom was coming toward me at eye level like a giant baseball bat, and I was the fastball. I let go of the sail and vaulted to my right, managing to keep my head from getting knocked off. But the end of the boom caught me on the funny bone with a crack. Groovy got the boom under control, and Joe and I dragged the big main back on deck. We all just lay there gasping in the rain, trying to figure out our next move.

"You're the fucking captain," Joe said to Groovy. "Got any ideas?"

"I think the rudderpost snapped, so the emergency tiller is useless. We've got to rig up some way to steer the fucker," Groovy said.

I could barely move my swollen elbow, now as big as a navel orange. It hurt like hell. We hauled out the sea anchor and rigged it up to stop us from drifting in the direction of the Amazon River while we tried to put our heads together and come up with a plan. The lights of St. Martin were just visible behind us, but going to weather was out of the question. We had a lot of time to think.

The rain and lightning had moved off under the black cloud to the south, and we sat for a while not saying anything. The wind whistled through the rigging above our heads.

There is nothing like a huge arena of adversity to kindle the creative spirit, and we finally came up with a system to make the boat go in the general direction we wanted to be sailing. Joe remembered a time he had been in a similar situation off the coast of Guatemala, and we used a combination of the auxiliary engine pushing us downwind and a small storm jib moving us upwind. We hoped we would wind up somewhere between St. Croix and Puerto Rico. With any luck at all, we might get to Tortola—but not in eight hours.

Our speed was now about three knots over the water, and our little overnight sail had turned into a two-day ordeal. Joe stayed on his watch, and Groovy got me a couple of pain pills for my elbow. I went back and lodged myself in the bunk, trying to ignore the steady throb in my elbow. It had continued swelling and was now the size of a grapefruit.

The whack to my elbow must have awakened the dormant hangover I thought I had avoided. Between that and the pain pills in my stomach there was no way I could sleep. Instead, I found myself topside with my head between the lifelines and my arm in a sling making fish food. Still, as sick as I was, I kept thinking that if all this misery passed, and I didn't die from cancer of the elbow, I wasn't interested in two-day-old pâté as my first meal. So I asked Groovy to save me a drumstick from the remaining chicken.

During that entire day we didn't sight a single other boat or even pick up any radio conversations between boats. We were alone in the Anegada Passage, and for good reason. The wind had intensified, and bands of thunderstorms were moving west toward Puerto Rico. This was not the kind of weather you saw advertised in the Virgin Island TV commercials.

We had no steering system, so we would sail until the jib luffed, and then we would turn the engine on, and the "iron geneoa" would move the boat downwind. We knew we were making headway because the radio station from St. Croix began coming in stronger, and we listened to the weather report: continued small craft warnings and near gale force winds.

Joe reminded me about Dr. Robby, a very fine cosmetic surgeon we'd met in Antigua. He ran a clinic in a big purple house on the hill where we were going. He was a sailing fanatic and had a beautiful little Herreshoff ketch that was a scaled down version of *Ticonderoga*, a boat I had always dreamed of owning. As soon as we docked we would find him and get my elbow examined. I stood watch and tried not to think of the pain; my elbow was now taking on a look and personality of its own.

By the end of the day, my appetite was back, and I started thinking about that chicken leg. But our captain had forgotten my request and scoffed it down. Pâté was not exactly what I had in mind for my first solid meal, so I nibbled crackers and hoped the wind would blow us to an island with a good restaurant.

Joe kept us amused that night with stories of one of his past lives—he had been a bull rider in the rodeo. The cowboys always scratched their heads when they announced him: "Coming out of chute number two, the Catskill Cowboy from Buffalo, New York, Joe Giovinno." I wanted to see a picture of Joe in cowboy getup. I'd only seen him in a T-shirt, shorts, and flip-flops.

I got over being mad at Groovy for eating the chicken leg. If our calculations were correct, we would see land the next morning, and I fell asleep repeating the names of good restaurants on all the islands we might hit.

I woke at sunrise to the smell of bacon. Groovy had

been feeling guilty about the chicken leg, and he was cooking us breakfast. He had found a half pound of bacon in the ice box and had scrambled up some eggs. It was one of the best breakfasts I had ever eaten. We ate in the cockpit, knowing the weather had changed, and the wind had dropped to about fifteen knots. The sky was finally beginning to clear, and in the distance we saw a group of small islands and located them on the chart. We had made it to the British Virgin Islands and felt ourselves to be quite the seamen.

We continued our steering routine and slipped through the pass between the islands into the Sir Francis Drake Channel. Road Town was in sight just a few miles to the north. Halfway across the channel, the temperature gauge on the engine was registering hot. Groovy asked Joe and me to take a look at the engine.

"If it is running hot, we'll just shut it down and fall off toward Virgin Gorda," he called out.

I went below and pulled the engine cover off. Joe followed me down.

"There's no way I'm going to Virgin Gorda," I said. I had seen the purple clinic on the hill, and I wanted to go see the doctor. Sailing to Virgin Gorda would take us the rest of the day.

Joe checked the water pump intake on the diesel. "These things are meant to freeze up before they blow up. Just tell him everything's okay."

"Everything's fine," I yelled up to Groovy. He waved back and smiled.

We steered up the channel and gingerly docked the boat at the Tortola shipyard. We figured people would be worried about us since we hadn't returned to St. Barts when we said we would. The dockmaster's mouth fell open when we told him we'd come across the channel with no steering at all. The word spread like wildfire around the harbor, and by the time we cleared customs, we had become legends. I was not interested in fame at the moment, and I headed up the hill to the clinic.

Dr. Robby wasn't surprised to see me. He, too, had heard about our crossing via the coconut telegraph, and he congratulated me on a fine piece of sailing. The last time I had seen him was in Antigua during race week.

I showed him my elbow and told him the story of how it happened. Then I waited for the bad news.

"Come with me," he said. He showed me into a large room where several women lay on stretchers covered with clean white sheets. Women came from all over the world to get overhauled at Dr. Robby's and spend a few weeks in the sun before returning to the accolades of their friends regarding their newfound youth. He took me into his office and pulled out a long needle.

"Is it cancer, Doc?" He inserted the huge needle into my elbow.

"Not at all, dear boy. You have a swollen bursa sack and a badly bruised tendon, but I'd say you're pretty lucky." He drained my elbow, and it returned to normal size. With the pressure of all the fluid gone, I could move it all the way up and down. Praise Jesus, I was cured.

We walked out through the recovery room, where yet another woman was lying. These were twentieth-century sleeping beauties. Dr. Robby would take no money, but we agreed to go for a sail in St. Barts soon.

It was a different day when I walked out of the purple

clinic on the hill. Having been healed, I was now happy to be a sailing legend. I met Groovy and Joe at the Village Inn, and we had our cheeseburgers and many piña coladas and relived the entire episode and toasted ourselves. People approached us to ask about the trip, and we told them.

Joe went on to St. Thomas on the seaplane that evening, and Groovy and I took a hotel room near the boat. We took long showers and slept in real beds under ceiling fans. The next day Groovy was at the shipyard tending to the steering problem, and I took off for home with two good elbows and a great tale to tell back at Le Select that evening.

JULY 10, 1987
Martha's Vineyard

I got word today that Joe Giovinno died in Honduras. I hope he was happy and had just come home from the bar bellowing his high-pitched laugh and flashing those wild eyes. He was in some jungle town in the Caribbean when his heart told him to get some rest. My old pirate buddies are disappearing like members of an endangered species, and as they go, our names move one more notch up the list.

I was feeling very mortal this evening. I drove to the airport, fired up my seaplane, the *Lady of the Waters*, and left the earth. I climbed up to eight thousand feet and headed to Provincetown, where I flew big circles around the part of Cape Cod that curls into itself like a giant fishhook. I cut the power and made a slow descent and flew along the beach just off the water, watching the swimmers wave. I found an isolated spot out of the wind and set the plane down and paddled up to the beach. I just sat there for a while in the shadow of the big sand dunes and said a prayer for Joe.

Joe Giovinno would take his beloved *Viking* from Provincetown to Tortola and across to Costa Rica and back up to Cape Cod as if he were just going around the block to get a newspaper. I thought about all the good times we had shared in the Caribbean. We had left a collection of rumors and innuendos scattered like shells on sandy beaches. I pushed away from the shore and let the breeze move the plane out to where I had a good take-off run and cranked up the *Lady of the Waters*. Soon the transition was made from boat to plane, and I turned south, back toward Martha's Vineyard. I was laughing aloud, thinking about that time when we crossed the Anegada Passage with no steering. None of what happened was very funny then, but it is now.